MW01616609

Puppy Smooches & Peppermint Kisses

Jennifer Faye

Lazy Dazy Press

Copyright © 2025 by Jennifer F. Stroka

All rights reserved.

No part of this publication may be reproduced, distributed, or transmitted in any form or by any means, including photocopying, recording, or other electronic or mechanical methods, without the prior written permission of the publisher, except as permitted by U.S. copyright law. For permission requests, contact [include publisher/author contact info].

The story, all names, characters, and incidents portrayed in this production are fictitious. No identification with actual persons (living or deceased), places, buildings, and products is intended or should be inferred.

Published by Lazy Dazy Press

Editor: Lia Fairchild

About this book...

WHEN SHE WAS A **child and wrote to Santa, she didn't know her wishes would come true years later...**

Holly Berry is spending her first Christmas without her grandmother, who had raised her. It's difficult, but she's getting through it. Then, unexpectedly, she's asked to foster a puppy. Feeling out of her depth, she turns to her childhood friend, who offers to give her some guidance.

Veterinarian Colin Bishop has given up on relationships after his busy practice keeps interfering in his private life. But when the girl-next-door needs some help, he's more than willing to make room in his busy schedule. But he knows not to fall for her infectious laugh or dazzling smile because his patients will always come first.

Holly never thought those long-ago Christmas wishes would come true, but ghosts from Christmas past have come to visit. Will Colin be able to bring the joy back to her holiday? Or will those ghosts ruin everything?

The Kringle Falls, Vermont, series:
Book 1 – *Puppy Wishes & Candy Kisses*
Book 2 – *Puppy Love & Snowflake Kisses*
Book 3 – *Puppy Smooches & Peppermint Kisses*
Book 4 – *Puppy Hugs & Mistletoe Kisses*

CONTENTS

CHAPTER ONE

THIS WOULD BE HER first Christmas alone.

It was just after lunch as Holly Berry stood in the storage room of the Kringle Soap Co. She opened a box of handmade snowmen-shaped soaps. She'd made them using one of her grandmother's recipes, which included things like coconut for the white ones, merlot for the red ones, and basil for the green ones.

Each year the store had a particularly popular item. This year it was the snowmen soaps and the bath bombs. And now she was running low on those items. Thankfully, business had been brisk this holiday season.

Even though there was a light snow falling outside, it was cozy in the shop. It wasn't just the warmth coming from the furnace; it was the warmth of friendship that flowed through not only her shop but throughout all of Kringle Falls.

The big difference this year was that Holly's grandmother wasn't there with her. The Kringle Soap Co. was her great-grandmother's creation. The shop had been in business for more than a hundred years. And now her grandmother had entrusted it to Holly to keep it going.

It wasn't until her grandmother had died that Holly realized just how much her eighty-one-year-old grandmother had done. The woman had been amazing, working straight up until the end. And now Holly couldn't let her down. She had to keep this place up and running.

"Holly." Her name was being called from the front of the shop.

"Just a second." She placed the box of soaps on the worktable. She would deal with them later.

When Holly stepped out of the back room, she found Merry Kringle standing in the middle of the store. Maybe she was there to pick out a gift basket for someone. Premade baskets with some extras such as bubble bath balls, loofahs, and some other whimsical items were new this year. Her grandmother had vetoed the idea in the past, but Holly knew with business in decline that she had to do something to boost the bottom line. And so far, the baskets were selling well.

"Hi." Holly sent her a smile. "Can I help you find something?"

Merry glanced at the soaps. "I've always loved this place." She made a show of inhaling one of the merlot soaps. "This whole shop smells heavenly."

Holly spent so much time in the shop she'd become immune to the scents. She stopped and made a point of inhaling deeply. "I never take the time to notice anymore." She inhaled again. "To me, it still smells like it did when my grandmother was here."

Merry nodded. "She would be so proud of you."

Holly hoped Merry was right. She had more ideas about changing the shop, but she wasn't ready to do anything so drastic just yet.

"Anyway..." Merry sent her a warm smile. "I'm sorry to disturb you."

Holly glanced around at the couple of customers that had just entered the store. "You're not. What do you need?"

"I hate to ask this of you..." Merry glanced down.

Holly had known the woman her entire life. Merry had been good friends with her grandmother. Gran used to tell her if she needed someone to rely on, and her grandmother wasn't around, she could call on Merry.

"That's okay." She wasn't used to seeing Merry looking so discomforted. "Just tell me what you need."

"It might be easier if I showed you."

"Excuse me," a teenager called from where she stood next to the checkout counter. She held up a container of unicorn bath bombs and some tea tree soap that could help with acne. "I need to check out."

"I'll be right there." She turned to Merry. "Can you wait a moment?"

"It might be more convenient if you stopped over at Purr 'n Woof after you close." Merry was out the door before Holly could agree.

That was strange. Really strange.

She glanced over her shoulder to see Merry hustling down the sidewalk. She couldn't help but wonder what was going on with her. Merry was normally a direct person. So, what had just happened?

Holly glanced up at the big clock on the wall. It would be at least four hours until she got an answer to that question.

A few hours later, Colin had only one more patient to see that day. If things went right, he'd get out of the animal clinic a little early. That didn't happen often. In fact, usually it was the opposite, and he ended up staying late.

He couldn't wait to leave. He had plenty of stuff to do at home. With it being the holidays, there always seemed like there was something to do.

"Looks like you're almost done, Doctor," Jane Estes, his office manager, said.

"Shh... Don't let anyone know, or they'll come up with something else for me to do." He sent her a teasing smile.

"Don't worry. I won't say a word."

"Is the last patient here?"

"No. They called. They're running a few minutes late because of the weather."

"No problem."

He moved to his office and checked his email. There wasn't anything there that couldn't wait until tomorrow. Now if only the last patient would arrive, he could leave early.

Ding.

He reached for his phone. There was a message from his brother Michael.

One of the puppies Candi was caring for has run away. Last seen at Merry Kringle's house. Escaped out of the back yard. No sign of him since.

His phone continued to light up with messages from his family. Everyone was going out, looking for the puppy named Tank.

Colin's fingers moved over the screen: *I'm at work, but I'll get the word out.*

He stepped out of his office and moved to the reception desk where everyone gathered at the end of the day. Jane, Mary, and Tyler were there. He told them the situation. And then he messaged his brother for a picture of Tank. He forwarded it to all of his staff.

"Where are they looking?" Tyler Jones asked.

"I think here in town. The puppy was at Merry Kringle's when he ran away. If you can just keep a look out on your way home, myself and my family would greatly appreciate it." He headed for the door.

"What about your last patient?" Jane called after him.

He paused in the doorway. "If they make it, call me."

He'd left his pickup in the parking lot. He wished he had a flashlight. Even though it was just after four o'clock, it was already dark out. He turned on the flashlight app on his phone.

"Tank!" He took his time, looking for little footprints in the snow.

He wasn't the only one out searching. He could hear numerous voices calling out for the puppy. Pride for his hometown swelled up in his chest. The people of Kringle Falls always pulled together.

Ding.

Ding.

His phone kept blowing up with messages from his family's group chat. Everyone was out searching. It was a good thing, because it had started snowing again. Tank was too young to be out in the snow for long.

A while later, after not finding any sign of the puppy, Colin's phone buzzed. He checked it for the umpteenth time. It was his mother warning everyone not to stay out in the cold for too long without taking a break. She was a worrier. She invited everyone home for some chili and fresh-baked bread to warm them up. He messaged back that he would stop by later. He didn't want to stop the search.

His phone dinged again. It was a message from his younger brother Justin. He'd checked the area around the Kringles' house and found no sign of Tank. Colin continued searching between the pet shop and the vet clinic. Still nothing.

Buzz.

It was the office. He answered, hoping that someone had brought in Tank. Instead, they were letting him know his final patient of the day had arrived. With a resigned sigh, he let them know he was on his way back.

Ding.

He checked his phone. It was a message from Candi: *Tank has been found. He's at home.*

Ding. Ding. Ding. Ding.

His phone started to blow up with more messages from family. It took him a moment to see there was a message for him. Michael wanted him to come over and have a look at the pup. He messaged back that he would be over as soon as he saw his last patient. He turned and walked as fast as he could through the new snow without falling.

Buzz.

He reached for his phone. When he saw the caller ID, he pressed the phone to his ear. "Mrs. Kringle, what can I do for you?"

"First, I told you a million times to call me Merry. And second, I need your help."

"If this is about Tank, I heard he was found."

"It's such a relief that he's okay, but this is another matter. If you could come over to the store, you'll see."

It wasn't the first strange phone call he'd received about a pet in trouble, but as far as he knew, Merry didn't have any pets, which was odd since she owned a pet store.

"I can't right now. As soon as I finish up with a patient, I'm headed over to my brother's to check on Tank."

"Oh, yes. Of course, I understand. What about a little later this evening?"

He wondered why she was being so insistent. "I'll do the best I can."

"Thank you. I knew I could count on you. See you later."

The line went dead before he could say anything else. So much for his early evening to get caught up on things.

Chapter Two

THE WORK DAY WAS done.

Holly yawned as she finished counting her receipts. It had been a good day—a very good day. Too bad all the days weren't like this one.

With everything secure, all she had to do was lock the door and turn off the lights. She started toward the exit. Before she reached it, the door flung open. Felicity Wright walked in. Holly's mouth gaped. She hadn't seen Felicity in a long time.

Holly rushed up to her with a smile on her face. "You're back."

Felicity smiled and nodded. "I am. I'm sorry I've been gone so long. Life gets busy in New York City and time goes way too fast."

"I totally understand." After Gran passed, the days blurred from one into the next. "How's life in the big city?"

"It's okay."

Felicity had left Kringle Falls for college and then got a job with a big publisher in New York City. Sometimes, Holly was jealous of her friend for getting out of this small town and being able to start over somewhere else. Other times, Holly couldn't imagine living anywhere but Kringle Falls.

Holly gave her friend a quick hug. "How long are you back for?"

"I'm not sure." When Holly sent her a curious look, Felicity said, "I mean, definitely until Christmas, but I don't know if I'll leave then or after the New Year."

"Well, it's good to have you back, even if it won't be for long."

Felicity looked around at the shop. "This place looks good. Your grandmother would be so proud of you." Then Felicity got a somber look on her face. "I'm so sorry I didn't make it back for the funeral."

"It's okay. I totally understand. The flowers you sent were beautiful." When her grandmother first passed, Holly had been in such deep grief that she wouldn't have been fit company. This was a better time for them to catch up. "I hope you'll have some time so we can get some coffee and talk."

Felicity nodded. "I should have some time when I'm not working at the bookshop."

Holly's brows rose. "You're back there?"

Felicity glanced away. "Connie could use some help for the holidays." There was something in her tone that seemed off, but Holly couldn't figure out what it was. "And, uh... It's not like I have anything else to do while I'm here."

Another odd response. "I thought you'd be spending your time visiting with your mother. She had to have missed you a lot."

Felicity's gaze lowered as she nodded. "I didn't tell her I was coming home. I thought I'd surprise her. The surprise was on me because her calendar is full between work and the holiday events. And I've missed working at the bookshop."

"I bet Connie is already trying to talk you into staying on."

Felicity shrugged as she lowered her gaze. "She hasn't said much about it. Well, I don't want to keep you. I just wanted to say hey."

There was definitely something going on with Felicity, but she didn't seem ready to discuss it. Holly understood. She hadn't been able to discuss what happened to her grandmother for the longest time.

"I'd offer to get coffee now"—Holly thought of Merry Kringle's request—"but there's something I have to do."

"I understand." Then Felicity stepped forward and gave Holly another hug. Without another word, she headed out the door.

Holly stood there for a moment, staring at her friend's retreating back. That was strange. What was up with Felicity?

Ding.

She reached for her phone and glanced at the new message.

Merry: *See you soon! *smiley face**

Holly sighed. This was turning out to be a very odd day. Not a bad one. Still, it was like there was something in the air—and she didn't mean snow.

But now her thoughts shifted to Merry's unexpected invitation. Holly couldn't help but wonder what Merry wanted and why she hadn't just told her while she was at the shop. Then again, Holly recalled that their conversation had been interrupted by a customer. That was probably why Merry had put off speaking to her.

After bundling up and turning off the lights, she headed out the door. The snow lazily drifted downward as she pulled the key from the lock. As soon as she turned, she realized what she'd forgotten to do—plug in the Christmas lights in the picture window. Nearly every store and home in Kringle Falls was decorated. She had to do her part.

She unlocked the door and went back inside. She moved toward the wall and grabbed the plug. She pushed it into the socket, and the window came to life. A smile tugged at the corner of her lips.

Once back outside, she inspected the display. There was a four-foot Christmas tree with multi-colored lights and various soaps for decorations. Beneath the tree were assorted baskets to give the shoppers ideas of how to create their own presents for that special someone in their life.

All the customers needed to do was wrap the basket and place it under the Christmas tree. People loved them. In fact, she might put more baskets together later that evening. It was why she couldn't spend that much time with Merry.

Although, she couldn't deny her curiosity about what Merry wanted with her. Perhaps it had something to do with the Kringles' annual Christmas party. It was that weekend. Holly wondered if Merry needed someone to bake some more cookies. Or maybe she needed someone to help her decorate.

Instead of turning right and heading to the entrance to her second-floor apartment, she turned to the left. The sidewalk was illuminated by the street lamps. There was a gentle breeze that picked up some of the fresh snow. It rushed the snowflakes into the air, swirled them around, before they kissed the ground.

The Christmas lights were on in all of the store windows, including hers now that she'd remembered to plug in her Christmas display. She loved this time of the year. It felt like Kringle Falls was a little bit nicer and the world was a little bit more compassionate.

She said hello to friends and strangers alike. She thought of swinging by the Kringle Cup Café to get a latte, but she decided to go to Merry's place first. She'd find out what she needed, and then she'd get her latte. It'd be an added boost to get her through that evening's chores.

It had been a busy day that ended on a good note. But he wasn't done yet.

Colin Bishop walked into his backyard. In the corner of the property was a large shed that he'd converted into a makeshift barn. It was home to Cupcake, the pig. Cupcake had been abandoned by her owners. They hadn't realized that "miniature" pigs when fed properly would weigh over one hundred pounds. Cupcake had been starved because the owners had been trying to keep her small.

Cupcake didn't live in the little barn alone. Her roommate was Jinx, the billy goat. Jinx had endured a spinal cord injury early in life. Colin had saved him from being euthanized. And now Jinx was getting used to his wheelchair.

Even though Colin lived in the borough of Kringle Falls, his backyard still resembled a small farm. Before he'd purchased the property, he'd had a conversation with the town mayor, Kris Kringle. Colin had explained how he would be taking in some animals here and there to help rehabilitate them.

Kris had praised him for his endeavor. However, it was pointed out that he couldn't have a barn in town. Colin gave it a little thought and came up with the idea of a shed. Kris agreed. When Colin mentioned a large shed, Kris told him that as long as the structure was indeed a shed, he could have whatever size he wanted.

He'd known when the Anderson place came on the market that it was the perfect place for him. The big white house had red trim and was in need of some TLC. He was working on the house a little at a time. He'd spent the bulk of his time working on the yard and the shed.

He believed his calling on this earth was to help animals. He'd never met an animal in need that he didn't want to help. He rehomed as many animals as possible. In the event that he couldn't find them a proper home, he took them home with him. At a later date, he might find a home for them. But there were special cases such as Jinx, who would stay with him permanently.

It was dinner time for Cupcake and Jinx. He fed Jinx first, just like he always did. Cupcake had no patience at all and started fussing.

"Cupcake, calm down. I'll be right there."

Once he finished with Jinx, he picked up the bucket holding pig feed and chopped fresh vegetables. She loved her food. He opened her pen and found that she'd overturned her feeding trough.

With a sigh, he turned to put the feed bucket down outside the pen. No sooner had he placed the bucket on the floor than Cupcake ran up behind him. Her head hit him in the backside. He went flying forward with his arms outstretched.

He landed on the concrete floor. His head rammed into Jinx's pen. With an *ugh* he sat up.

He gave his head a quick shake before looking over at Cupcake. If a pig could snicker, she was doing it. She had merriment dancing in her eyes.

And then she eyed up the bucket. He moved faster than she did. He shoved the gate shut. Cupcake let out a frustrated sigh.

He eyed her over the gate. "Are you going to behave?"

Cupcake let out a snort. He wasn't quite sure what it meant.

"If you behave, I'll feed you."

Her gaze moved to the overturned trough. He took his time opening the gate again, keeping an eye on her as he moved. Cupcake stood still, as though she knew if she moved, it would be that much longer until she got to eat.

He turned over her trough. She just watched him. And then he dumped the bucket into it. He knew from past experience to move posthaste after dumping her food, or he would get mowed down. Nothing stood between Cupcake and her dinner.

At lightning speed, he stepped outside the pen. He closed the gate and secured it. He peered over the gate and watched as Cupcake snuffled down her dinner. A smile pulled at the corner of his lips. Two months ago, she was emaciated, and he wasn't sure she would make it. Now she was beginning to put on some weight. It was taking time, but she was beginning to look healthier. By springtime, he hoped she'd be ready to go live on a farm.

He turned to Cupcake and Jinx. "Sorry. I have to go. I'll check in on you guys later."

And then he headed outside where there was a light snow falling. He had been planning to start stripping the wallpaper in the dining room, but it had waited a couple of years now. It could wait a little longer.

Right now, he had a house call to make at his brother's place. And that was to be followed by a stop at the pet store to see what was on Merry Kringle's mind. Perhaps she'd found a stray animal out in the snow. The thought quickened his footsteps as he ran inside to collect his medical bag and be on his way.

CHAPTER THREE

WHEN HOLLY ARRIVED AT Purr 'n Woof, she saw the Closed sign in the window. She wondered if Merry had gotten tired of waiting for her and left. When she tried the door handle, it moved, and the door swung open.

Holly stepped into the shop and closed the door behind her. "Hello?"

There was nothing but silence.

She stepped farther into the shop and raised her voice. "Hello?"

"Holly…" Merry walked toward her from the back. "I'm glad you're here." She waved at her to follow her. "We're in the office."

We? Who is we? Holly followed her. She had to say that her curiosity was piqued.

Holly came to a halt at the doorway. When she saw Dr. Colin Bishop, DVM, her heart lodged in her throat. In her childhood and teens, he'd been the boy-next-door. He was a few years older than she was, and she'd had the biggest crush on him. Of course, he never noticed that she hung on his every word. Nor did he complain when she would follow him around as he cared for his pets.

When he was a teenager, he'd mow her grand-mother's grass. In the winter, he'd shovel the driveway and sidewalk. He was somehow always around.

Even though she was too old to write letters to Santa by the time she fell for him, it didn't stop her from wishing each Christmas that he would see her as a young woman and not the kid who used to follow him around. However, her Christmas wish never came true.

After he went away to college and then vet school, they'd drifted apart. When he returned to Kringle Falls a couple of years ago to open up his own veterinarian office, her life was busy working at the soap company. Each year, she took on more responsibility to lighten the load for her grandmother. Sure, they'd see each other in passing, but their interaction was never more than a hello.

She swallowed past the lump in her throat. "Hey, Colin."

He glanced up from where he was petting a white puppy with large brown spots. When Colin's brown gaze met hers, her heart launched into her throat just like it used to do when she was a teenager. A smile lifted the corners of his lips, and his dimples were on full display. She swallowed hard past the lump in her throat.

Colin was no longer a lanky teenager that she remembered. Now he was all muscle and attitude. His brown eyes turned dark as though camouflaging his secrets.

He was a man with a history she knew nothing about. And it made her wonder what had happened to him in the past fourteen years—not that she'd ever find out.

"Hi, Holly. It's great that you're fostering this puppy." He sent her an approving smile.

What is he talking about? Her gaze moved to the puppy sitting on the desk. She was supposed to foster him? *No.* He had to be confused.

"There must be a mix-up, because I'm not fostering him."

Merry stepped forward. "Sorry for the confusion." Her gaze moved to Colin. "I haven't had a chance to ask her yet."

"Oh." His brown eyes widened. "Sorry."

In that moment, Holly felt as though she'd stepped in a trap. Her instinct was to leave, but her thoughts were jumbled. She couldn't come up with a legitimate excuse.

"Holly." Merry's voice softened. "I could use your help. I need a home for Tater Tot."

Cute name. But this isn't happening. Holly's wide-eyed gaze moved to the puppy on the desk and then back to Merry. "I... I can't. I don't know anything about dogs."

"Oh." Merry sent her a reassuring smile. "I think you'd do an amazing job. Don't you think so, Colin?"

He turned his attention from the puppy to Holly. "Definitely. I remember how she was always good with my dogs when we were kids." Then he gestured for her to step closer. "Come say hi."

Her feet of their own volition stepped closer to Colin...and the pup. She had no idea what they were up to, but there was no way she was taking that puppy home with her. Even if he was cute and had big almond-shaped brown eyes that could melt even the coldest of hearts. Still, she had to stand her ground.

She just had to tell them it wouldn't work. Yet, when she opened her mouth, she said, "He's so cute."

Now why had she gone and said that? It would only encourage those two to further their agenda. Still, as she stared at the puppy, she couldn't deny her words. He was cute, and he was going to make someone a great pet, just not her.

"Go ahead," Colin said. "You can pet him."

She glanced over and saw Merry watching the interaction. Holly's attention returned to the pup. It wouldn't hurt anything to pet him. Because who doesn't like puppies and want to pet one?

She reached out, and the puppy jumped back, away from her reach. Well, that wasn't the reaction she'd been expecting. She yanked her hand back as a frown pulled at the corners of her lips.

"It's okay," Colin said. "He doesn't know you, so you have to move slow. Slowly raise your hand and hold it out so that he can get your scent."

She didn't think this would work, but what better way to prove to them that she wasn't the right person to foster him. And so, Holly raised her hand and held it out there. Tater Tot looked at her hand, but he didn't move, not a single solitary step.

"Now, call him," Colin said.

Really? Couldn't they see this was hopeless? Apparently they didn't get the point that she wasn't good with animals. She swallowed. "Tater Tot."

"Not like that," Colin said. "Put a little enthusiasm in your voice. You know, like you're going to play with him."

"But I'm not."

"But you could try." Colin arched a brow at her, just like he'd done all those years ago when they were kids, and he'd bring her over to play ball with his dog Moose.

That dog had been almost as big as her. She had been scared to death of him, though she didn't tell Colin that. She'd wanted him to like her, and she knew he loved all animals, both big and small.

Moose hadn't been your typical dog. He had problems walking, and eventually Colin's family had to get Moose a wheelchair for dogs.

But as she looked at Tater Tot, she realized she had nothing to fear. Tater Tot was just a little dog, one that was made for cuddling. Something told her Tater Tot was more afraid of her than she was of him.

And so she tried again. This time she took her time so as not to startle him.

"Talk to him," Colin coaxed. "Let him know that you want to be his friend."

Holly cast Colin a frown. She knew that much. When she turned back to the puppy, she wore a smile.

"Hi." She tried to keep her voice soft. "I'm Holly. I just want to pet you. I promise I won't hurt you."

As she talked to him, she continued to move her hand forward. Tater Tot's little white tail swished back and forth like a windshield wiper on overdrive. And then at last, her fingertips touched him. His fur was smooth as she petted him. All the while, he was staring at her, as though trying to decide if he should trust her.

When she went to pull her hand away, Colin said, "Here." He got to his feet. "Sit here and keep petting him. Let him get used to you."

After she was seated, she gazed up at Merry's smile and Colin's creased brow. She had to dispel this notion they had that she would be taking Tater Tot home. "He's a sweet puppy, but I can't take care of him."

Colin's gaze met hers. "I remember how you used to be afraid of Moose."

"I was not." The denial rushed from her mouth, causing Colin to arch a brow. She huffed. "Fine. But he was as big as a real moose."

A half-smile lifted the corner of his mouth, taking her back in time. That was the way he'd look at her when she would try to show off for him. Back then, she'd have done anything to get his attention. She'd even considered getting a dog, knowing how much Colin loved them, but her grandmother shot down the idea. It was probably for the best. Holly wasn't good with animals. The cautious look Tater Tot gave her was evidence of that.

While she was still looking at Colin, she felt something wet and cold on her hand. She turned her head to find Tater Tot had moved over to sniff her. And then he ran his smooth tongue over the back of her hand. She didn't know what to do, so she sat still and let the puppy do his thing.

"See. He's just giving you puppy smooches." Colin smiled.

She sat there, letting the puppy sniff her and lick her. In return, she petted him. By the time she was ready to leave, she was holding Tater Tot. His warm little body felt good in her arms.

She liked the little guy, but she had reservations. "I still don't think this is a good idea."

"It won't be for long," Merry said. "I would take him home, but Kris is allergic to dogs."

Before she could stop the words, they came flying out. "But you own a pet store."

Merry smiled as she nodded. "The store came before the husband. And it worked out because this way, I get to be around animals every day without it bothering Kris. I guess you could say I get the best of both worlds."

"Oh." She hadn't been expecting to hear that Kris was allergic to animals. But still, sending Tater Tot home with her wasn't the best idea. "Are you sure there isn't someone else who could take him in?"

When her gaze landed on Colin, he held up his palms. "Don't look at me. My place is already full of animals. It's starting to look like a petting zoo. I don't want to run afoul with the mayor."

She wasn't giving up. "Surely there has to be someone else."

"It won't be for long," Merry reiterated. "Please. I wouldn't ask if it wasn't urgent. The other puppies he'd been living with have already been adopted, and I don't want to leave him in the store overnight all by himself."

Holly glanced around. The store was big and with the lights out, she could imagine how scary it would be for a puppy.

"And I'll help you out as much as I can," Colin said.

She wanted to take comfort in his words. "But you're so busy with the veterinarian office."

He nodded. "But I'll give you the number to the bat phone."

His *Batman* reference made her laugh. It brought back memories of him wearing *Batman* T-shirts. It had been a long time since she thought of that.

He frowned at her. "What are you laughing about?"

She sobered up. "I didn't know you still liked *Batman*."

"Of course, I do. He's unbeatable."

She smiled again as she shook her head. The puppy rubbed his head against her chin. Maybe she wasn't so bad with animals after all. Or maybe she was just deluding herself. She smothered a laugh.

When Holly glanced up, she found Colin and Merry sending her an expectant look. She was starting to feel as though she didn't have a choice.

"It won't be long," Merry said. "Just a night or two."

Holly glanced over at the puppy. He was cute. Then the reality of the situation settled in. "But I have to work."

"Take him with you," Merry said. "I'm sure your customers will love to see him. He might even find a home that way."

Holly searched for another reason this situation wasn't going to work. "I don't have anything for him. No food. No nothing."

"No problem." Merry moved off to the side. Behind her was a little table with a big brown paper bag plus a bunch of other stuff, including what looked to be a fluffy bed.

It looked like these two had put their heads together and tried to head off her reservations. She had to admit that they were persuasive.

She tried to come up with any other reason this was a bad idea, but she struggled. A silence settled over the room, as though they were waiting for another objection. But what was it? She was certain there was another reason this was a bad idea.

And then it came to her. "It's snowing outside, and I didn't drive. You don't want the puppy out in the snow."

"No problem," Colin said. "I have my pickup. I can give you a ride home."

She frowned at him. He wasn't supposed to keep solving her problems. All he did was smile back at her.

At last, she felt as though she'd lost the battle. She turned to the puppy. She reached out and petted him. His tail swished back and forth across the desktop. "You can come home with me, but it's only temporary. Okay?"

Tater Tot's tail continued to swish.

"I'll take this stuff out." Colin collected the supplies from the table.

As Holly took in the magnitude of what Merry had collected for her, she thought it was an awful lot of supplies for just a night or two. But Merry distracted her as she gave her tips about the pup's feeding schedule and potty breaks. Holly tried to memorize it all, but there was so much, and her mind was still trying to come to terms with the fact that she would be taking care of a dog.

Now that her grandmother had passed, she'd been forced to sell the only home she'd ever known and move into the apartment above the soap company. Even though it had been five months since her grandmother's passing, Holly would still forget and rush into the storage room in the back of the store to tell her grandmother something. When she would find her grandmother's stool at the work table empty, the sense of loss would wash over her again.

Maybe Tater Tot would be a good distraction. Even though his stay would only be temporary. This arrangement was just for a night or two.

Needing reassurance, Holly looked at Merry. "This is just for a night or two at most. Right?"

Merry nodded. "I appreciate this."

Colin entered the office after his second trip to the pickup. "Everything is ready to go."

Holly's stomach shivered with nerves. She didn't want to mess this up.

CHAPTER FOUR

HAD THEY DONE THE right thing?

Colin had been surprised when he showed up at Purr 'n Woof Supplies and found Merry with Tater Tot. When Merry said she couldn't take him home because of her husband's allergies, Colin thought she was going to ask him to take the dog. As it was, he had three dogs and one cat in the house, plus the goat and pig in his backyard barn.

He truly did worry about alienating Merry's husband, the mayor. Colin couldn't afford to let that happen. He was happy living in town, close to the clinic. But on a practical side, he couldn't afford to sell his house and buy a farm out in the country. He definitely didn't have time to run the animal clinic and take care of a farm. No way.

But when Merry mentioned Holly, his ears had perked up. Growing up, she had been the girl-next-door. When she was little, she was an annoying shadow, but as she'd matured into a beautiful teenager, his feelings toward her had warmed up. But she was three years his junior, and when you were young, those three years made a big difference, so he kept her at arm's length.

Now, Holly was all grown up, and even though he didn't think it was possible, she grew more beautiful every day. And it wasn't the makeup, because she hardly wore any. It was just her goodness that started on the inside and glowed outward in her smile and the twinkle in her blue-gray eyes.

He couldn't believe all of the puppy things he'd loaded into his pickup. Merry had gone overboard, but he wasn't saying a word. He knew if Holly backed out of taking care of the puppy, it would fall on his shoulders. Everyone in Kringle Falls knew he had a soft spot in his heart for animals. The sadder their story, the more he opened up his heart.

But he knew Holly—well, he used to know Holly—and she had a big heart too. He thought about how he'd failed to renew their friendship in the last two years since he'd moved home. It weighed on him. That was why he decided he'd help her to feel confident in her ability to care for Tater Tot.

After loading the remainder of the puppy supplies into the pickup, he closed the door and headed back into the back of the pet shop. When he stepped into the office, he found Holly sitting at the desk petting the puppy. It looked like this transition was going to go smoothly.

"Everything is loaded." He approached Holly. "Are you ready to go?"

She got to her feet and looked at Merry. "You'll let me know as soon as you find a home for the puppy?"

Merry nodded. "I will."

Holly wrapped her fingers around Tater Tot and picked him up. The pup's tail wagged as she snuggled him against her chest. Colin wondered if that puppy was already home in Holly's arms.

He was usually good at making light conversation, but as he escorted Holly to his pickup, he found himself struggling to think of anything to talk about.

As they stepped outside, he said the first thing that came to mind. "Looks like snow."

He inwardly groaned. *Really?* That was the best he could come up with?

And so, as he helped her with the dog to get into the pickup, they talked about the weather. The weather. *Seriously?* He was better than this.

When he pulled out of the alley, he automatically turned right.

"Hey," Holly said, "you turned the wrong direction. I live above the soap company."

"Oh, yeah. Sorry. It's an old habit." He slowed the pickup to a stop at the next intersection. What was going on with him? He put on his turn signal.

Until recently, Holly had lived in her grandmother's house next door to his parents' place. After her grandmother died, the house had been sold. His parents were unhappy to see Holly move.

He honestly hadn't even known there was an apartment above the soap company. He never knew of anyone living up there. He couldn't help but wonder what condition it was in after being vacant for countless years.

A couple of minutes later, he pulled to a stop in front of the soap company. He looked at the showroom window and smiled. "I like your display. It's very festive."

"Thanks." Her voice was hesitant. "It's the first time I did it on my own."

He could hear the pain in her voice. He reached over and squeezed her forearm. "I'm so sorry about your grandmother. Every time I visit my parents, I glance over at your grandmother's house and expect to see her rocking on the front porch."

"The new family... They have young children. They'll, um...make the house a home."

His hand was still resting on her arm. "I'm sorry you had to move."

She didn't look at him as she shrugged. "It was time."

She adjusted the puppy in her arms. When she moved, his hand fell away. He wondered if that had been the intent of her movement.

He turned off the engine and got out. He made his way around to her door. A glance in the window let him know that Holly was struggling to hold the puppy, keep her hand on the leash, and release her seatbelt.

He took his time opening the door so as not to let the puppy escape. However, Tater Tot didn't seem to want to go anywhere. He seemed quite content on Holly's lap. Colin couldn't blame the pooch. Holly was pretty great.

When he had the door open, he asked, "Do you want me to take him for you?"

"Uh, yes. Thank you." When she handed Tater Tot to him, she paused to unwrap the red leash from her hand.

He had nothing to worry about. From the marks on her hand, she had a very firm hold on him. It was sweet the way she worried about the puppy. Merry had been right about having Holly care for the puppy.

With Tater Tot in his arms, Colin stepped back. When she stepped out of the pickup, her foot hit the sidewalk. One moment she was standing next to him, and the next moment, she was falling. With lightning speed, he reached out to her. His free arm wrapped around her waist and drew her to him. She landed against his side with an *ompf!*

He turned his head in her direction. When she tilted her head upward, he realized just how close she was. If he were to lower his head, their lips would meet. He wondered if her kisses were as sweet as he was imagining.

At the last second, he realized his head had moved ever so slightly toward her. *Whoa!* What was he doing? He stopped and turned toward the squirming puppy. Hopefully, Holly hadn't noticed that he'd momentarily lost hold of his faculties.

She straightened. "So sorry about that."

He swallowed hard. "Are you all right?"

"Yes." She reached into her purse. "I'll unlock the door."

He followed her to the single door next to the soap shop. She had to stab at the lock a couple of times before she got the key in and opened the door. She stepped inside and flicked on a light.

She pulled the door wide open. "Here. I can take him."

"That's okay," Colin said. "I've got him."

She hesitated, as though she weren't sure what to say. The longer she stood motionless, the more he got the impression she didn't want him to see where she lived. Why would that be?

Maybe he was reading too much into the situation. Perhaps she'd gotten shaken up when she almost fell on the ice.

Holly turned and headed up the stairs. At the top was a door. She opened it and stepped inside. He followed her. He wasn't sure what he expected to find, but it wasn't a wall of cardboard boxes.

He took a couple more steps between boxes. He couldn't tell if she was still unpacking or if she'd changed her mind and was moving out.

Once he stepped past all of the boxes, he entered the kitchen. It was like he'd gone back in time. The clash of colors was the first thing he noticed. There was faded yellow-gold wallpaper on the walls. The cabinets were mint green with no backsplash and a scarred butcherblock countertop. The white laminate table with chrome legs was paired with red vinyl chairs.

And if that weren't enough, the floor was done in black and white tile. It had cracks here and there along with a lifetime of scuffs. This kitchen had seen a lot of life but not recently.

Drip...

Drip...

Drip...

His head turned toward the white porcelain sink, and he noticed the faucet was leaking. The yellow-green refrigerator, with a big dent in the bottom door, turned on. The compressor made a loud rumbling sound. It didn't sound like it had much life left in it.

Oh boy! He had no idea this was how Holly was living. When he caught her gaze, she frowned at him.

He opened his mouth to say, well, he wasn't sure what to say, but before he said anything, Holly held up her palm. "Don't."

"What?" He was confused. He hadn't done anything.

"Don't tell me how sorry you are or whatever it is you were going to say." She leveled her shoulders and tilted her chin upward ever so slightly. "I don't need your sympathy."

"That wasn't what I was going to say."

She arched a disbelieving brow. "You weren't?"

He shook his head. "I was going to say that I'm in the process of renovating my house."

"You are?"

He nodded. "The place is ancient, and the owners before me didn't do a whole lot of work on the place."

"Oh." She blinked, as though she were computing his words. "Why did you buy it?"

"Because it comes with a double lot, and that is hard to find in Kringle Falls."

"Oh." And then she looked guilty. "I'm sorry for jumping to conclusions. I guess I'm just a little self-conscious about the place. I'm saving up to hire some contractors."

He nodded. "Let me know if you need any recommendations."

"I will. Thank you."

The puppy was squirming in his arms. "Where do you want me to put him?"

"Uh." She glanced around. "Anywhere. I guess."

He hesitated. "You might want to keep him contained for a while. You know, until he gets acclimated to your place, and you're sure that he's housebroken."

Her eyes widened. "I hadn't thought of that. I tried to tell you and Merry that this wasn't a good idea."

"It'll be fine." He glanced around. "You'll want to keep him away from carpeting and rugs until he hasn't had any accidents for a couple days."

"He won't be here that long." She frowned. "Shouldn't he be housebroken by now? He's what? Six months old?"

"Merry told me he's three months, so he's probably still in the process of being housebroken."

"Oh. Well…" The frown on Holly's face returned. "Obviously, there's no carpeting in here, and I ripped it out of the living room."

"You're going to want to pick up anything that you don't want him to chew on or to play with, especially your shoes. And you're going to want to watch out for your garbage can because he'll attempt to be a dumpster diver if given a chance, and trust me, you don't want to clean up that mess."

He glanced around at the various items on the floor, including a laundry basket with folded clothes in it. There were some bottles of various cleaning fluids. There were also other things sitting around that would need to be moved out of the puppy's reach.

He felt sorry for her as she rushed around picking up everything. "How about I take him home?"

"No." She grabbed an empty box from the other room and started to fill it. "I'm the one who agreed to do this."

The dog squirmed in his arms. Colin ran his fingers over Tater Tot's back, hoping to calm him long enough for Holly to pick up things.

He wanted to help her, but first, he needed to do something with the puppy. He turned to Holly. "Can you hold him?"

"I'm picking up things."

"I understand. But I have an idea that will help you."

"Okay..." She put down the box of cleaning supplies, and then she turned to him with her arms outstretched.

Once he placed Tater Tot in her arms, he said, "I'll be right back. I have to get something out of the pickup."

A couple of minutes later, he rushed back into the kitchen to find Holly sitting at the kitchen table with the puppy still in her arms. Her fingers were brushing over the puppy's back. It looked like they were adjusting to each other.

"I got his crate." He carried it into the kitchen. "I'm just going to set it up here because he's going to want to be wherever you are. But later, you'll want to move it to your bedroom. He'll use it to sleep in at night. Make sure to place it next to your bed. He'll feel more secure to be close to you. This is all new to him, so he's going to be scared at first."

Her brow creased. "I need to do all of this, even though we'll only be together a day or two?"

"Even then." He had a sneaking suspicion they were going to be together a lot longer than a couple days.

Once Colin had the crate situated and they put the pup in it, he helped her clean up the kitchen and living room. All the while, she apologized for the mess. And each time he told her not to worry about it.

He could see that she'd been working on fixing up the place. She'd taken up the carpeting in the living room and put down a large area rug. And the walls looked as though they'd recently been painted a light blue-gray with white trim. The place was coming along, although probably not as fast as she would have liked.

She'd had him put all of the stuff in the front room just off the kitchen. He guessed at one point it was a dining room. Now it resembled a warehouse with boxes stacked literally to the ceiling. He wondered what was in the other boxes, but he didn't dare ask.

The one thing he noticed while helping her was that there weren't any Christmas decorations up. He found that odd since Kringle Falls was a Christmas town, and the holiday wasn't far off.

Maybe she didn't have time to decorate. He could understand that. He hadn't gotten out his decorations until the past weekend. Sometimes, there just wasn't time to do everything you wanted to do, and then you had to prioritize. He ended up prioritizing things more times than he would like.

At last, it looked like everything that could be a danger to the puppy was picked up. Now to block off the room with all of the boxes. "Do you have a baby gate?"

"What?" She looked at him like he'd just sprouted another head.

"Sorry. I wasn't thinking. Of course, you don't."

"What do we need it for?"

"To keep him contained in whatever room you're in." He glanced around. "Maybe two gates would be better."

"I don't know." She frowned, as though she felt overwhelmed by taking in the puppy. "How much are they?"

This is something he could help her with. "They are free. I have some extra at my place. I'll just run over and grab them."

"I don't know. I feel bad about all the trouble you're going to for me."

He waved off her worry. "Don't be. You didn't ask to have a puppy dumped in your lap. I'm glad I was around to help."

She turned to look at the puppy, who was lying on a fluffy blue blanket in the crate. "He is adorable. But I don't think I'm the right person to do this."

"You'll get the hang of it." He felt bad for her. She seemed so overwhelmed. He wondered why Merry had picked Holly, of all people, to take the puppy.

And then he had a thought. "Did you eat dinner yet?"

She shook her head. "I didn't have a chance. I went over to Merry's right after I closed the shop."

"How about I pick up a pizza?" When her eyes lit up and she nodded, he asked, "Pepperoni?" When she nodded again, he said, "I'll be back."

He headed out the door, into the snow. This certainly wasn't the evening he'd thought he'd be having, which consisted of a frozen pizza on the couch, surrounded by his dogs and cat while he watched television.

Instead, Merry's phone call had led him in an entirely new direction. It was a chance for him to reconnect with Holly. It seemed as though she could use a friend. He wanted to be that friend.

Chapter Five

THIS WAS NOT HOW she expected her evening to end up.

Holly sat at the kitchen table and sighed. She couldn't believe Colin had been in her apartment and had seen the mess. Just the memory had her face warming with embarrassment.

And the fact that he'd helped pick up stuff only caused her to feel utterly mortified. This was the guy she'd crushed on so hard in her teens, and the one time he visits her place, it looks like a bomb had blown up in it.

The truth of the matter was that ever since she'd lost her grandmother, she'd been struggling: struggling to pay the medical bills, struggling to move and sell the house, struggling to keep the soap company running just like her grandmother had done. And so when it came to this apartment, it fell last on her list of priorities.

The puppy whined, drawing her attention back to the present. Before Colin left, he'd brought in the boxes Merry had packed for her.

But first, she made walls out of boxes to keep the puppy in the kitchen. Once that was done, she turned her attention to the bag of puppy stuff. At this point, she didn't have a clue what was in it, but it looked stuffed full.

Who knew puppies needed so much stuff? It was like he was a tiny human. She dug through the items until she found a bag of kibble. Merry had been thoughtful enough to write a note for her, telling her when and how much to feed Tater Tot.

Holly got out his bowls. She washed them and filled one with cold water and the other with a quarter cup of kibble. Once the bowls were on the floor, she opened the crate. Tater Tot didn't come rushing out.

Instead, the pup sat there, looking at her like he wasn't sure what to do. She called to him, but he still wouldn't exit the crate.

Then she got an idea. She retrieved his food bowl and waved it near him. His nose started to go. However, when she called out for him to follow her, the pup wouldn't move.

After trying a couple of times, she finally gave up. She moved both of the bowls inside the crate. That seemed to do the trick because he immediately started to eat the kibble. She breathed a sigh of relief.

While the puppy ate, she cleaned and set the kitchen table for two. It was something she'd never done before in this place. She hadn't even had her friends Belle and Felicity over. She had a new friend, Candi, but she hadn't had her over either. She was too embarrassed about the place to have anyone over.

She had been so busy taking care of her grandmother's estate. She was appointed the executor. It wasn't that she was the only family her grandmother had. There were also Holly's parents, but they'd been MIA Holly's whole life.

Her grandmother had been angry with her parents for abandoning their nine-month-old baby and never looking back. But her grandmother had wrapped Holly up in love and been the best parent. She could be firm when needed, but she was also compassionate, and she had been Holly's biggest cheerleader. She always said that together they could accomplish anything. Holly would suppose that was true.

And now that the estate was settled except for a few legal steps, she could turn her full focus back on the soap company.

Buzz-buzz.

It was the doorbell. Colin must be back with the gates. She rushed over to the stack of boxes. She shoved them aside to reach the top of the steps. By the time she made it, Colin had let himself inside and was making his way up the steps with his arms full.

When he reached the top steps, she offered to take the pizza box from him. She inhaled the aroma of tomatoes and oregano. Her stomach rumbled in anticipation. It appeared she was hungrier than she'd thought.

She squeezed past the boxes. "Sorry about those. I was using them as a wall so I could let the puppy out to eat, but he had other plans, so I let him have dinner in his crate." Then she wondered if she'd done the right thing. "That's all right, isn't it?"

Colin leaned the gates against the wall. When he turned to her, he had a smile on his face. "It's fine. Just relax. You have good instincts. Trust them."

"I don't know..." She worried her bottom lip. How could she have good instincts when she'd been abandoned by her mother and father? At that moment, her instinct was telling her she was doing everything wrong. After all, she'd never had a pet in her life.

"Seriously. You've got this." His voice had a reassuring tone.

She wanted to believe him, but she had so many questions and no answers. She supposed that when she curled up in bed that evening, she'd be conducting internet searches to answer some of those questions. But it was only for a day, two tops. It was like a mantra she kept repeating in her head.

"I'll just set up these gates." Colin's voice interrupted her thoughts.

"I have the table set." And then she had a thought. "Unless you'd rather have pizza in the living room."

He paused from where he was setting up the gate to the living room and sent her a lazy smile. "I don't remember you being this unsure when we were kids. In fact, I remember a very determined young lady." His smile broadened. "I remember how you used to stomp your foot when you got frustrated. You were a cute kid."

Heat rushed up her neck and settled in her cheeks. She refused to look at him. "I don't remember any of that."

It wasn't exactly true, but she didn't want to continue talking about how embarrassing she was as a kid. And she didn't want him to stumble down memory lane so he could recall the gigantic crush she'd had to him.

"You don't? Because I certainly do." When he paused to stare deep into her eyes, it sent her heart racing. "That cute kid blossomed into a beautiful woman."

The breath hitched in the back of her throat. He thought she was beautiful? She resisted the urge to run her hand over her honey-brown ponytail to make sure it wasn't falling out. She could just imagine errant strands of hair going every which way. By evening, her hair had a mind of its own.

She turned away, not wanting him to see the effect his words had on her. She turned on the faucet and released a pent-up breath. He didn't mean it when he said she was beautiful. He'd just said it off-handedly. That had to be the explanation. He was just being nice.

She squirted some liquid soap on her hands. Even if he did mean it, why was she letting his words get to her? She'd gotten over him a long time ago. Right now, she had to focus on taking care of Tater Tot.

A noise from the dog crate had her wondering if the pup had read her mind. She subdued a laugh at anyone reading her mind. At times, it could get scary in her brain.

Forcing her thoughts back to Tater Tot, she realized she didn't want to mess things up with the puppy. Even though she'd just met the pup, she'd fallen under his charming spell. How could she not? He was adorable. She was certain Merry wasn't going to have a problem finding him a home.

She dried her hands and moved to the fridge. She pulled the door open and scrounged around inside to see if she had anything to make a side salad. She had a partial head of lettuce, but she didn't have any vegetables to go with it.

It was obvious she never entertained guests. *Ugh!* She was turning out to be a horrible hostess. And then she picked up the bottle of salad dressing. There might be enough for one bowl of salad but definitely not two. A trip to the market moved to the top of her to-do-list.

Chair legs scraped across the hardwood floor, jarring her out of her meandering thoughts. She closed the fridge and turned around.

"Holly?" Colin's voice once again drew her from her thoughts. "Did you hear me?"

He'd said something? The heat rushed back to her cheeks. "Sorry. What did you say?"

"Would you like me to get the drinks?"

Her gaze moved to the table where Colin had already served the pizza on each of their plates.

"I've got it." She moved to the fridge and opened it. The shelves were practically bare. This was getting embarrassing. "I'm afraid I can only offer you water."

"Sounds good to me."

Thankfully, she was on top of the dishes. She withdrew two tall glasses from the cabinet and filled them with faucet water. With it being winter, the water was very cold, so there was no need for ice.

Feeling embarrassed that she didn't have anything else to offer him, she placed the glasses on the table and then sat down, keeping her gaze lowered. This whole evening had been so stressful.

And then she noticed Tater Tot had finally meandered out of his crate. The pup stopped between them. She smiled down at the little guy. Tater Tot's head turned back and forth between her and Colin. The next thing she knew, the pup put his paws on Colin's leg. It seemed Tater Tot had made his choice. Not that she could blame him. Colin was like an animal whisperer.

While Colin fussed over the puppy, she took a bite of her pizza. It was delicious. She hadn't splurged on takeout since her grandmother was alive. Since then, there had been a lot of ramen noodles, box mac-n-cheese, and spaghetti.

"Are you planning to put up any Christmas decorations?" Colin asked.

She looked over at him and couldn't help but laugh. "Have you looked at this place? The last thing on my mind is Christmas decorations."

His brows rose. "Are you trying to tell me that you aren't going to have a Christmas tree?"

She shrugged. "I don't know if I'll have time to put one up."

He nodded. "I understand. Sometimes life doesn't slow down so we can get off the ride."

"The ride?"

"You know, whatever situation has your full attention."

"I suppose now that I'm off the settling-the-estate ride that I need to hop on the unpack ride."

"It's okay to ask your friends for some help."

She shrugged as she reached for another piece of pizza. "It's just that everything happened so fast with Gran. One moment she was fine, the next she was in the hospital. And then... Well, you know. And after I lost her, there were so many things I had to take care of for the estate. Now, well, I'm just trying to sort out things for myself."

"What about your parents? Have they been around to help you?"

She stared down at her uneaten piece of pizza. "They were too busy to make the funeral. They had some business meeting. Can you believe that? They didn't want to reschedule. They said it was too important—more important than Gran's funeral. Then again, I shouldn't be surprised. They were too busy to raise their own daughter."

Sympathy shone in Colin's warm-brown eyes. "I'm sorry."

She shook her head. "You have nothing to be sorry about. You made it to the funeral home. And you're helping me now. It's so much more than my parents ever did for me."

She pressed her lips together to silence her mouth. She couldn't believe she was talking about her parents. They were not something she talked about with anyone—including her grandmother.

"When I was young, Gran tried to cover for them to explain away their absence," Holly said. "As I grew up, I figured out Gran was making excuses for them to make me feel better. It didn't work. So, we agreed not to discuss them. Ever. What was the point? They were never coming back. And that was fine with me."

Maybe it hadn't been fine with her younger self—the child in her that longed for a mother to take her shopping for a dress to wear to the school dance, for a father to take her to the father-daughter dance.

"I'm sorry, Holly. They missed out on getting to know a very special person."

She blinked as she remembered when she was a kid and Christmas would roll around, and she would write letter after letter asking Santa to bring her parents back to her. Each Christmas morning her heart would be filled with hope that they would be sitting in the living room next to the Christmas tree.

And each Christmas morning, she would be disappointed. She didn't understand what was so wrong with her that her own parents didn't want her. Gran always said there was nothing wrong with her—it was her parents that had something wrong with them.

But all of that had been a long time ago. As a kid, Holly had figured out that going forward, all she needed was Gran. But now her grandmother was gone too. So, Holly figured the only person she could count on going forward was herself.

Something cold touched her arm, jarring her out of the past. She glanced to the side and saw Tater Tot sitting there, staring up at her. He was so cute, and she could use a hug right then.

She leaned over and picked him up. As soon as he was in her arms, he turned and licked her face. She wasn't expecting that. His tongue was smooth against her skin and left a wet trail up her cheek.

"Those are puppy smooches. Get used to it," Colin said. "I have a feeling he's going to be giving you a lot more."

Puppy smooches? It was a cute term.

When she put the pup down on the floor, she resisted the urge to wipe away the wetness from her cheek; she didn't want Colin to think that she didn't like the puppy. The truth of the matter was that she had no intention of liking or disliking Tater Tot. Liking the puppy meant she'd care about him, and if she cared about him, she'd want to keep him, and that was not happening. Nope. Not her. She was fine on her own.

"What's wrong?" Colin's voice drew her from her thoughts.

"Uh, nothing. Why?"

He shrugged. "You just had this look on your face. I couldn't tell if you were... Never mind."

Holly glanced over at the puppy and gasped. "Stop!"

"What's wrong?" Colin struggled to turn around.

"The puppy is peeing. Correction: he just peed on the floor."

A dimpled smile came over Colin's handsome face. When she frowned at him, he burst out laughing.

"This isn't funny," she said in her most indignant tone.

"If you could see the look on your face, you wouldn't say that." He laughed some more.

She continued to frown at him.

When he sobered up, he said, "I'm sorry. I forget that you aren't used to being around animals. Why is it that Merry asked you to take care of Tater Tot?"

"Your guess is as good as mine. I mean, almost anyone else in Kringle Falls would be a better choice than me."

"I don't know about that. You have a big, generous heart. That's all Tater Tot needs."

Holly focused on the puddle in the middle of her kitchen. "I thought Merry said he was potty trained."

"I think you mean house broken. And I believe he is."

"Then why did he do that?" She pointed to the mess.

"Because sometimes when dogs are stressed or not feeling well, they can revert in their training. You just have to get him back on track."

"I do?" Her voice rose an octave. "But I don't know the first thing about housebreaking a dog." She sighed. "I'm thinking I should call Merry and tell her that I made a big mistake by agreeing to take him."

"Nonsense." Colin got to his feet. He glanced around. "Where's the bag of puppy supplies?"

She pointed toward the outer room with all the boxes. "I didn't want the puppy to get into it."

Colin nodded in understanding before he headed out of the room. A few seconds later, she heard a bit of rummaging around.

He reappeared with a white bottle in his hands. He held it up so she could see the label. "Use this when the puppy has an accident."

"Oh. Okay."

Together, they cleaned up after the puppy. Colin let her know that she might want to set a timer and take the puppy out every hour until they settled into a routine. Holly insisted they wouldn't be together long enough to form a routine.

Colin slipped on his coat. "And now I have to go. I have my own furries that need me to look after them." He paused and looked at her. "Do you want me to take Tater Tot with me?"

Yes. Definitely. But when she opened her mouth, something quite different crossed her lips. "No. I've got this."

"Are you sure?"

No. Not at all. She nodded. "Yes." It was then that Holly realized she had taken up his entire evening. "Thank you for everything. I feel a little more confident about this venture."

"Don't worry. You're going to do great. Also, I noticed Merry left you lots of helpful notes. And she included a puppy guide book. It should help you with the basic questions.

"Oh. Okay. I'll look at that tonight."

"Can I see your phone?" He held his hand out to her.

She didn't know what he was up to, but she trusted him. She retrieved it from her back pocket and handed it over. He ran his fingers over the screen and then handed it back to her.

"There. You can call me any time."

"Even if it's a silly question like what time does he go to bed?"

"There are no silly questions when caring for an animal. And the answer would be when he falls asleep. Puppies his age have high energy and have to recharge. So, probably around eight or nine o'clock his energy will run out. Make sure you wake him up for one more trip outside before you crate him for the evening."

She looked down at her phone and checked the time. She had a bit before she could put him to bed. And then she remembered she was supposed to set a timer to remind herself to take him outside. "How long did you say to set the timer for his next potty break?"

"Well, Tater Tot is a few months old so he can hold it a little longer. You could start with an hour."

"I can do that."

After Colin disappeared into the snowy night, Holly turned around to Tater Tot. "Looks like it's just you and me. Maybe I should look in that bag of supplies and see what other goodies Merry sent home with us. And then I'll set up your bed next to mine. Okay?"

The puppy gave her a wary look.

Holly hoped this arrangement went better than she'd imagined. Maybe she should have taken Colin up on his offer to take the puppy with him. Because she had absolutely no idea what she was doing.

CHAPTER SIX

HOW HAD HE LET their friendship lapse?

The next day, Colin couldn't help but smile every time he recalled his evening with Holly. He wondered how she was making out with the puppy. Throughout the day, he'd given thought to calling her, but before he could turn thought into action, he was called away for a consultation or emergency at the animal clinic.

Now, with his workday over, his thoughts drifted back to Holly. It was no wonder she didn't have any holiday decorations up, since it looked like she was still in the midst of moving in. It was almost like she wasn't planning to stay, but he knew that wasn't right. After all, where would Holly go? She'd been born and bred in Kringle Falls. She wouldn't leave. Would she?

After broaching the subject of her parents, it was obvious she wouldn't be going to see them. What had he been thinking to bring up the subject of her parents? It was a well-known fact that her parents had abandoned her as a baby.

He never saw her parents. They could walk right up to him, and he wouldn't recognize them. Sadly, he wondered if it was the same way for Holly.

And worst of all, Holly had lost the one person who was solidly in her corner. Guilt assailed him. Sure, he might have gone to her grandmother's funeral along with most of the town, but afterward, he should have been a better friend to Holly. He should have been there to give her a shoulder to lean on while she'd gone through those monumental changes in her life.

He was a pro at procrastination. He would tell himself he was too busy building up his clinic. He also would assure himself that he'd stop by and check on her another day. The only problem was that "another day" never came. He was done with all of the excuses and justifications.

The clinic closed at five o'clock, and he tended to a few walk-in emergency appointments before he walked out the door. He went straight home to check on his own furbabies. Everyone was happy to see him and even happier to get their dinner. And then he thought of calling Holly, but he decided that seeing her in person would be better. So, he went over to her place.

It wasn't until he was ringing her buzzer that he felt as though he shouldn't have shown up empty-handed. A moment later, the door swung open. Holly stood there with her hair in a messy bun, an old T-shirt and gray sweatpants on.

Her eyes momentarily widened. "Colin, what are you doing here?" She ran a hand over her hair before tucking a stray lock of hair behind her ear. "I mean, hi. Do you want to come in?"

He nodded. When she moved back, he stepped into the entryway. He closed the door against the winter air and followed her up the stairs.

As he climbed the stairs, he couldn't help but think she was the most beautiful woman he'd ever known. Once they were in the kitchen, she turned to him. Her face was flawless, except for a bit of flour on her cheek. His fingers tingled with the need to reach out to her, but he resisted the urge.

But when he took a second glance, he noticed the shadows beneath her eyes. She was tired. Maybe he shouldn't have stopped over.

"If you're busy," he said, "I can go."

"No, silly. You're already here. So, stay."

He wasn't going to argue with her. "I hadn't heard from you today, and I was wondering how things were going."

Ding. Ding. Ding.

"That's my timer. I have something in the oven."

While she took care of the oven, he slipped off his coat and hung it over the back of a kitchen chair. The apartment was warm and cozy. There was a hint of a buttery sweet scent in the air. Whatever she had in the oven, he definitely approved of.

He also noticed there appeared to be fewer boxes in the other room. He took that as a good sign. If she had time to do a bit of unpacking, things with the puppy must be going all right.

Before he could find out what she was baking, Tater Tot ran over to the gate separating the kitchen and living room. He was barking with his tail wagging so much that his whole backside was swaying side to side. He had a good heart and would make someone a great companion. He just wondered if Tater Tot's sweetness would melt through Holly's resistance to keeping him.

Colin moved next to the gate and bent down. "Hey, boy." He reached out and petted the dog. "Are you being a good boy?"

"As long as you don't count him having accidents in the house." Holly sighed as she came to stand next to him.

"I'm sorry. Once he gets comfortable here, he'll do better."

"But he's not supposed to stay long. I thought Merry would come for him today, but when I called her, she said the family she had in mind didn't work out. Do you know how hard it is to run a shop and take care of a dog?"

His brows rose. "You took him to work with you?"

"Well, yeah. I couldn't just leave him home alone." Then she sent him a worried look. "Why? Wasn't I supposed to do that?"

"It's fine. I was just surprised. You, uh..." He wasn't sure how to phrase this without upsetting her. "You just seemed so unsure about having him around."

"I took his bed and attached his lead to the counter. So, he was out of the way. When he was asleep, the customers didn't even know he was there."

Colin was afraid to ask the question, but he just had to know. "And what happened when he was awake?"

"He yapped until I got him. The customers all scooped up soap to purchase so they could come up to the counter and meet him. All they could do was fuss over him. I tried to find someone to adopt him, but none of them were interested. They all had one excuse or another. But I sold a lot of soap. A whole lot."

Colin smiled. "See there. You have a new sales associate."

"Is that what you call him?" She looked at Tater Tot and shook her head. "Even so, I think it'll be better for him to find his 'fur-ever' home sooner rather than later."

"And so, you're helping the process?"

She shrugged. "I'm doing what I can. I told everyone to spread the word that he's available for adoption, and they offered to help. Some even took a picture of him."

There was a part of him that was hoping Holly would adopt Tater Tot. Colin couldn't help but feel with her grandmother gone, Holly needed someone in her life. And as he knew from experience, a dog can make a great companion. Maybe what she needed was a bit more time.

He couldn't shake the feeling that Merry had been doing a bit of matchmaking when she paired Holly with Tater Tot. A little smile tugged at the corners of his mouth. It seemed to be working out, whether Holly wanted to admit it or not.

"What are you smiling about?" She arched a brow.

He didn't know that his thoughts had translated to his face. He glanced around the kitchen. "It looks like you've started a bakery." He arched a brow. "Did you go and change the soap company to a bakery?"

"No, silly. This is for the Kringles' Christmas party this weekend."

His gaze scanned the kitchen. "She asked you to bake all of this?"

He knew Merry was concerned about Holly with this being her first holiday alone, but asking her to not only care for Tater Tot but also to bake, what? Six different types of cookies seemed like a lot.

"She didn't ask me to do it. I volunteered."

He was still taking in the dozens and dozens of cookies. "But why?"

"My grandmother did all of this for Merry's party each year. I thought I would keep up the tradition. It's what Gran would have wanted."

He wondered if her grandmother would want her granddaughter taking on more responsibility. She had more than enough going on in her life with moving into a new place while keeping the soap business operating.

Colin opened the gate to let the puppy in the kitchen. Tater Tot ran over and jumped up on him. Colin leaned down and petted his head. "Hey, boy."

"Tater, get down." Holly's voice had a firm tone to it. When the pup got down, she said, "Good boy."

Colin was impressed. "Looks like you've been working on your training."

"It was in the book Merry put with the supplies. I read it last night."

"As in you read the whole book last night?"

She nodded. "I needed to know what I'm doing."

He was impressed. Maybe the pup was the best medicine for her. But with all of this baking, he worried that she was overdoing it. He might have to have a word with Merry.

His gaze moved to the sink and the surrounding counter. There was a pile of mixing bowls, spatulas, and baking sheets. He might not know much about baking, but he could definitely help load the dishwasher.

The timer went off. While Holly got two trays of cookies from the oven, he rolled up his sleeves. He moved toward the sink.

Holly straightened and looked at him. "What are you doing?"

"I'm going to work on that stack of dishes."

Her gaze moved from him to the overflowing sink and then returned to him. "Oh, no. I've got it."

He was pretty certain that after working all day and then baking all of this, not to mention taking care of the puppy, that she was exhausted. "I don't mind pitching in. I'll have this cleaned up in no time."

Once he had the dishwasher filled with the first load, he'd see what Holly wanted to eat for dinner. He glanced around. It was then he realized there was a hitch in his plan.

There was no dishwasher. *Oh no.* He'd just volunteered to handwash all of this stuff. He inwardly groaned.

"Is there a problem?" Holly's voice jarred him out of his shock.

"Uh. No." *Yes. Definitely yes. How is it that she doesn't have a dishwasher?*

"The dish soap is under the sink. You don't know how much I appreciate this. I never realized until now how busy my grandmother was in order to run a business, raise me, and still participate in community events. She was impressive."

"So are you." He located the soap and a dishrag. Holly had a drying rack, so he supposed that was something. Then again, with all these dirty dishes, there was no way they'd all fit in that drying rack. He hoped she had a lot of dish towels.

He got to work. He found himself continually glancing over his shoulder to see what Holly was up to. They chatted about the snow, the holidays, and his family.

When he glanced over at her and noticed a piping bag in her hand, he lowered the dish rag. "What are you making with the piping bag?"

"The butter cookies. I pipe out the dough in order to make all of the ridges. When they come out of the oven, I'll take half of the cookies and dip half of each one in white chocolate. The other cookies, I'll dip in milk chocolate. Then I'll add red, white, and green nonpareils." When he sent her a puzzled look, she clarified. "Round sprinkles."

"Oh." He nodded and gave it some thought. "I remember those cookies because I always thought they looked like they would take a lot of work to make."

Holly continued piping the cookies. "They take a fair amount of time, but they are totally worth it."

"I'm looking forward to having one, if you're willing to share."

"I suppose that's the least I can do for the help." When she smiled at him, he got a funny feeling in his chest.

He briefly smiled back before returning to washing more dishes. There were two large mixing bowls in the sink and one on the counter with frosting. He wanted to ask how many mixing bowls she owned, but he didn't.

They continued to work. She dirtied the dishes, and he cleaned them. He'd swear that she dirtied them faster than he could wash them. By the end of the evening, he knew his way around her kitchen.

He wanted to stay and have dinner with her, but he couldn't do it, because he had his own furbabies waiting at home for him. And then he had an idea.

"Would you like to come to my place for dinner tomorrow?" he asked.

Holly hesitated as her gaze moved around the kitchen where almost every flat surface was covered with cookies.

Before she could turn him down, he said, "Come on. You know that you need to eat. And Tater Tot can meet my dogs. The socialization will do him good. I'm sure he's missing the other puppies he traveled here with."

"I hadn't thought of that." She looked at Tater Tot, who was now lying next to her feet. "Okay. If you're sure it's not an imposition."

"It won't be." And then they made arrangements for the following evening.

When he left, he told himself it wasn't a date. They were just two old friends helping a stray dog. Nothing more.

CHAPTER SEVEN

SHE WASN'T SURE WHY she'd accepted his invitation.

The following day, Holly was a nervous wreck. She'd dropped things, forgotten things, and knocked things over. Thankfully, her customers were too distracted by Tater Tot to pay her clumsiness much attention.

The pup practically glowed with all of the attention. It made her happy to see him doing well, even if she was still struggling to figure out what he needed when he would bark at her or sit there and stare at her with his head cocked to the side.

As soon as she locked the soap company's door for the evening, Holly raced upstairs to get ready for her date...um, for her dinner with... *Nope.* That sounded too much like a date too. She was getting ready to eat dinner at Colin's house. *Yes. That's it. Finally.*

This was her first visit to Colin's house. She'd heard that he'd bought the place on the edge of town, but she didn't head in that direction very often, so she hadn't checked it out. And now that she was on his street, she realized that in the daylight, he would have a spectacular view of the distant hills.

With Tater Tot curled up on the passenger seat, she turned into Colin's driveway. The first thing she noticed were all of the twinkle lights strung across the front of his house. It was festive-looking but not something she would have expected from Colin. Maybe she didn't know him as well as she thought she had. Or maybe Colin had changed a lot since they grew up.

His walks were shoveled, except for the little bit of fresh snow that had fallen that evening. On the porch was an inflatable brown dog wearing a red Santa hat and a matching red scarf. It was cute and rather fitting.

On the other side of the red front door was an inflatable Christmas tree that must have been six feet tall. Tater Tot wasn't sure what to make of the blowups. He sat up in her arms and growled at the tree, never taking his gaze off of it.

When she knocked at the door, a chorus of barks started on the other side of the door.

Tater Tot's growling grew louder.

"It's okay." She petted him. "You're safe. And those dogs are going to be your new friends. It's okay. You're okay. We're okay."

The barking stopped, and then the front door swung open. Colin smiled at her. "I'm so glad you made it."

"Thanks for the invite."

She could see past him. There were two, no...make that three dogs behind him. One looked to be a brown lab. The second was a white mid-size dog. Maybe a bull terrier. She wasn't sure. And the third one looked to be some sort of St. Bernard mix.

Colin took a moment to fuss over each of them. The tails were going like crazy. And then he made them sit. She was impressed with how well they listened.

Tater Tot stopped growling as he watched the other dogs. She petted him, hoping to calm him.

She stepped inside, not sure what to expect. Tater Tot smashed himself against her chest as he looked down at the other dogs while they stared up at him.

"It's okay," Colin said. "They won't hurt him."

She hesitated. "Are you sure? They look so big compared to him."

"He'll be fine. I promise." Colin's voice was soft and soothing, like she remembered when they were kids. "They are used to having various animals pass through the house."

She recalled when they were kids how he had tried numerous times to get her to pet one of his stray pets. They weren't always dogs or cats. *Oh no.* Colin didn't discriminate when it came to loving animals. He loved them all, including toads and snakes. *Ugh!* She drew the line at snakes and spiders. *Eww!*

His current adoptees were cute and fuzzy, not creepy, crawly, or scaley. Still, they were awfully big. She continued to stand there with Tater Tot clutched to her chest.

"May I hold Tater?" Colin held his hands out to her.

She hesitated. She knew she was being silly. Colin was the one person she trusted above anyone else in this town. She handed over Tater Tot. Then she wasn't sure what he wanted her to do.

"Go ahead. Pet the dogs."

She looked at the dog closest to her. He was the biggest of the bunch. He was the one that looked as though he had a lot of St. Bernard in him. It was only then she noticed his back legs were on wheels, like a wheel chair. *Aw... Poor baby.*

"This is Thor. He's in charge." Colin's gaze moved to the dog. "It takes a lot of work to keep those other two pups in line, huh?"

Thor barked once, as though he was in total agreement.

She couldn't help but smile. Her pulse raced as she held out her hand. Thor sniffed her before approaching her. He moved on his wheels as though they were a part of him.

Crouching, she ran her hand over his head. The next thing she knew, he was licking her cheek. She hadn't been expecting that.

"See." Colin smiled. "I knew he'd like you."

She smiled. "I like him too. Can I ask what happened to him?"

Colin nodded. "He has hip dysplasia." When she sent him a confused look, he said, "His hip joint didn't develop properly. So, he needs a little help getting around."

"He seems to do well on the wheels."

"You should see him run around in the back-yard." Colin nodded to the side. "And next to him is Spuds." When she went to move to Spuds, Colin rushed on to say, "Wait. You need to know that he's deaf."

"Oh no. Poor baby. What happened to him?"

"He was born that way. So, with him you have to be careful not to startle him. You want to make sure he can see you at all times, and when you touch him that you do it gently."

"I can do that." She held her hand out to Spuds, and he licked it. She couldn't help but smile. "He seems nice."

"He's a big baby. Even though he's deaf, I still talk to him. He can feel the vibrations from our voices." Colin shrugged. "I just like to think it helps him feel more connected."

"Hello, Spuds. You're a sweetie." While she spoke, the dog's tail thumped the floor.

She talked to him as her hand ran down over his short white fur. In the background, she could hear Tater Tot whining. Was it possible he was jealous? Surely not. They hadn't been together long enough to form that sort of bond. It was more likely he just wanted some attention too.

She turned her attention to the chocolate lab. "And who are you?"

"This is Harley. He's very playful."

As the dog sat before her, she gave him a quick onceover. He looked healthy. "Do I need to be aware of anything with him?"

"Harley? No, he doesn't let his handicap hold him back. He's an overgrown puppy."

She gave Harley a closer look, noticing he was missing a leg. *The poor baby.* "He looks healthy to me."

"He is very healthy. But he got tangled up with a car and lost one of his back legs. He doesn't let that stop him. He runs and wrestles as well as his four-legged counterparts. Sometimes, I think he's even more agile."

She knelt down and introduced herself to Harley as she held out her hand for him to sniff. "It's nice to meet you."

The next thing she knew, Harley lathered her face with puppy smooches. She was caught off-guard and there was something else. It took her a moment to figure it out. And then it came to her—she was touched by the dog's sweetness.

"I forgot to warn you that Harley is a bit of a lover." Colin stood off to the side, still holding Tater Tot. When she stood, he asked, "Do you trust these guys with Tater?"

Her immediate answer was still no. Tater was so small next to them. They could trample him without even knowing it. She knew that she was being overprotective. And this acknowledgment shocked her.

She'd never been overprotective in her life. There never had been an occasion for her to be overprotective of another person or animal. *Wait.* Did that mean she was forming an attachment to Tater Tot?

No. That couldn't be it. Because he wasn't staying. Merry was finding him a home, and then what would happen to her? She couldn't lose anyone else she cared about.

Nope. She wasn't going to let the silly little pup into her heart. It wasn't going to happen.

And so she deferred the question to Colin. "You're the expert. What do you think?"

He arched a brow. "You want me to make this decision?"

Her heart beat a little faster because she knew what Colin's decision would be, and it made her nervous. Still, she couldn't let herself get attached. "Yes. You decide."

"Okay. I think Tater Tot will be fine with the other dogs. After all, he came from a shelter where he was around a lot of other dogs bigger and smaller than him. And then he traveled here with Tank and Odie. I think he'll do fine." He paused, as though waiting for her input.

She bit back all of her worries, and she was surprised by how many she had. Instead of speaking and giving those worries a chance to escape, she merely nodded her head.

Colin knelt down and placed Tater Tot on the ground next to him. Keeping the leash short, he let Tater Tot decide what he wanted to do. For a second, the pup stood still as he stared at the other dogs.

Then Tater Tot ambled over to Harley. They attempted to sniff each other. When Harley moved to sniff Tater's butt, Tater scampered away and ran head first into a wall of fur, otherwise known as Thor. Tater Tot bounced back from the big dog and landed on his butt.

Tater lifted his head. A confused look appeared on his little face as he tried to figure out who he'd run into. Then he barked at Thor. Tater barked some more.

Holly grew concerned. "Why is he barking?"

Colin smiled at her. "It's okay. He wants Thor to play with him."

"Really? But Thor is huge compared to him."

"Apparently, Tater disagrees."

When Thor wouldn't play, Tater moved on to Spuds. They immediately hit it off. They raced into the living room. It was the first time she paid attention to the details of the room.

It was a spacious room with big windows and a fireplace at the end of the room. There were two large couches and an armchair. In the corner stood a tall pine tree. It was trimmed in red and white decorations.

Her gaze moved from the tree to Colin and back again. "Did you decorate the tree all by yourself?"

"Uh, yes." He cast a worried look at the tree. "Why? Is it that bad?"

She shook her head. "It's that good."

Just then Tater and Spuds stopped in the middle of the room. They were fighting. *Oh no!*

Holly's chest tightened. "Hey, stop!"

When she went to rush to his aid, Colin held out an arm, stopping her. "He's okay. This is how they play."

"Play?" That sure didn't look like playing to her.

Poor Tater Tot was on the ground, belly-up, and it looked like Spuds was biting him. That wasn't playing.

Colin lowered his arm. "I promise they're fine."

She glared at him. "I thought you knew all about dogs."

"I do." He nodded toward the dogs. "Look now."

When she turned her head, she found Tater was standing, and it was Spuds on the floor with his feet in the air while Tater stood over him. It still didn't look like playing to her.

"Trust me. They'll let us know when the playing gets too rough. One of them will let out a squeal of pain."

"I think that's enough play for now." She scooped up Tater Tot, who complained about being picked up. She ignored his protests as she held him safely in her arms.

She took a moment to take in the living room. It was very comfy. She could easily imagine curling up on one of the couches with the fireplace warming the room as she watched a Christmas movie on the large-screen television. And then Colin's image appeared, and he was seated on the couch next to her.

She gave herself a mental shake. Where had that come from? Her crush on him had ended years ago—back when he left for college. He was yet another person whom she'd cared about and who had left her.

But she didn't want to think about any of that right now. Colin was being her friend. He was trying to help her and Tater Tot. Their friendship deserved a second chance.

Chapter Eight

THIS WAS A MISTAKE.

Holly was feeling overwhelmed from her worry over Tater Tot's safety to the resurrection of old memories. And yet there was no graceful way to make a quick exit.

She was stuck there for the duration. She just needed to get herself together and stop thinking about the past.

Colin pulled out his phone. "I'm going to order from the Mistletoe Diner. Do you have a favorite?"

She shook her head. She didn't have the extra money to splurge, but she wasn't going to let him pay for her. The shop brought in enough to get by on, but she wasn't rolling in money. And right now, every extra penny she got, she planned to put into the renovations of the apartment.

"Do you like rosemary chicken or pot roast?" he asked.

"The chicken sounds good."

"Perfect." He dialed the restaurant.

While he placed the order, she walked over to the bookcases that flanked the fireplace. There weren't that many books. Most of the ones on the shelf were veterinary medicine reference books. Most of the shelves were filled with framed photos of animals: cats, dogs, a pig, a goat, a miniature pony, and a rabbit.

When Colin was off the phone, she turned to him. "Are these pictures of your patients?"

"No. Those are my furbabies."

Her eyes opened wide as she looked around the room for some sign of them. "You have all of them?"

He let out a hollow laugh. "No. They aren't alive any longer."

"I'm sorry. I should have figured it out." When Tater Tot wiggled in her arms, she looked at him. "You're getting heavy."

"You must be feeding him well."

She shrugged as she lowered Tater Tot to the floor. "I'm just following Merry's instructions. By the way, have you talked to her today? I tried to call her earlier, but I couldn't get a hold of her."

"And you're wondering if she found someone to take in Tater Tot?"

"Uh, yes." She watched as Tater Tot made his way over to Thor. They sniffed each other, and then Tater Tot started jumping around, barking at Thor. "Should I stop him?"

Colin shook his head. "He just wants to play. See his tail wagging. Why are you so anxious for Merry to find him a new home?"

Holly shrugged. "It's just not fair to him to get used to living with me and then to shuffle him to another home."

Colin looked over at the tail-wagging pup. "I think he's going to be just fine."

She wanted to believe him, but she knew how important stability was to youngsters. And even though Tater Tot wasn't human, she still believed this was true. She wanted the best for the pooch.

"Mrr..."

Holly turned her head to see an orange, black, and white calico cat stroll into the room. The cat walked over to Colin and rubbed against his legs. The cat's purr was so loud Holly could hear it.

"And this is Clementine."

The cat strolled over to her and rubbed over her ankles too. "She's very friendly."

"Yes, she is." He moved to her side.

She knelt down to pet the cat. It was only after she'd pet the cat that she noticed Clementine was missing an eye. The poor baby. And part of her ear was missing. *Aww...*

It didn't stop Holly from wanting to scoop her up and take her home. But of course, that wasn't necessary because she was certain Colin spoiled all of his furbabies, including Clementine.

When Holly straightened, Clementine jumped up and leaned against her leg. Holly scratched her head. When the cat didn't seem to be going anywhere, Holly scooped her up into her arms.

As she petted the cat, she chanced a glance at Colin. He was keeping an eye on the dogs. Tater was sniffing his way around the room.

"Do you mind if I ask what happened to Clementine?"

"No. She was a stray that was brought into the clinic. She was sick. Her eye was infected. The eye couldn't be saved."

"And her ear?"

"They do that when a feral cat is sterilized, and they release them back to the wild. Someone found her and dropped her at the clinic. They didn't stick around. And so I took her in. I wasn't planning to keep her, but there aren't a lot of people who want a one-eyed cat."

"And..."

His brow crinkled. "And what?"

"And you fell for her, didn't you?"

He smiled. "Yes. I did. She's the best. She puts up with the dogs. In fact, she bosses them around."

She looked at Clementine. "I bet they're a lot of work to keep in line. Huh, girl?"

"*Mrr..*"

"Don't let her tell you any big stories. We aren't that much work." Colin sent her a teasing smile. "Would you like to meet Cupcake and Jinx?"

"Who are they?"

"Well, I'll introduce you to them."

First, she couldn't believe she was there in Colin's home. It wasn't anything like she'd imagined. Then again, she had never imagined his home. She'd been too busy taking care of her grandmother and then herself.

Second, she couldn't believe he'd turned his home into an animal refuge. Actually, that part shouldn't surprise her. Colin always had the biggest heart when it came to stray animals.

Once Colin turned on some more of the interior lights, she was able to see a dining room to the left. It wasn't anything fancy. In fact, it looked like it was having some work done to it. There wasn't any furniture, only a bunch of drop clothes.

A smile pulled at the corner of her lips. It felt as though a weight had been lifted from her shoulders to know that she wasn't the only one who didn't have the perfect home.

Although, as she looked around, she realized that Colin was well ahead of her. But this was the sort of encouragement she needed to keep going. Because one day soon, her place would be completed, and hopefully, it would look warm and cozy like his place.

"When I got the place, I knew it was going to be a fixer upper. I just didn't know how much work it would require."

"You've done an amazing job fixing it up."

"Thanks. It's a constant work in progress."

"That's how I think of the apartment."

"Don't worry. Before you know it, you'll have it looking just the way you want."

She wanted to believe him. She truly did. It was tough living out of boxes. "I was thinking after the New Year that I might shorten the number of days a week the shop is open or shorten the hours. I'm still debating it. Anyway, it would give me more time to work on the apartment."

"If you need a hand, just ask."

"Thanks, but I know how busy you are."

"Speaking of which." He gestured for her to follow him. "Let's go."

"What about Tater Tot?"

"You can bring him with us, or you can leave him with the others."

She looked at the other three dogs. Although they looked adorable, she wasn't sure she trusted them alone with Tater Tot. "I think I'll bring him."

They grabbed their boots from next to the front door and carried them to the back of the house. While she slipped on her boots, Colin stepped outside and grabbed the snow shovel. He cleared the fresh snow from the porch steps.

When she joined him, he shoveled the walkway to what she could only describe as a small red barn. She searched her memory, but she couldn't recall ever seeing it before. "Was this always here?"

"No. I built it last year."

"Wow. You're talented. Maybe I should hire you to remodel my apartment."

He stopped in front of the door to the little red barn. He turned to her. "I can help you, but..."

"No." Heat rushed to her cheeks. "I didn't mean that. I... I was joking. I mean, uh... I know you could do it because you are talented. I was, uh..."

He smiled at her. "Holly, it's okay. I know what you meant. But I wouldn't mind helping you."

It took her a second to realize he was serious. "I'll keep that in mind." She peered into the building. "Wow. It looks like a real barn in here"

"I did my best." He glanced back at her. "You can put Tater Tot down. He'll be safe in here."

She took him up on the suggestion. The pup wiggled in her arms. As soon as Tater Tot's feet hit the ground, he was sniffing everything. He reminded her of a blood hound as he smelled everything around him.

Holly stepped up next to Colin. "And who do we have here?"

"This is Cupcake." He went on to explain how she'd been rescued a few months ago. "We've been working through some issues."

Holly stepped up to the pen and leaned over. Not knowing what to expect, she saw a skinny pig. "Poor baby."

Holly held out her hand to the pig, but Cupcake was just out of reach. While Holly was trying to make friends with Cupcake, Tater Tot was walking around, pulling on his leash every chance he got. She glanced down to check on him. He didn't seem to be getting into any trouble...at the moment.

While she'd been distracted, the pig moved to the other side of the pen. There were a couple of scars on the pig's side and thigh. She thought about inquiring about them but decided some things were better not known.

"She's a little shy," he said. "We're working on it."

Holly enjoyed meeting Colin's animals. She noticed how each of them had some sort of imperfection—then again, didn't we all? Still, Colin found a way to help them. He was still a hero just like he'd been when they were kids. The only thing he was missing was a cape.

When she went to turn to the other pen, her body moved but her feet didn't. There was something wrapped around her ankles. But with her body in motion, she couldn't stop what had already been put in motion. The next thing she knew, she was falling.

Large hands and strong arms reached out to her. Colin yanked her toward him. Her palms came to rest against Colin's muscled chest.

When she raised her head, her gaze met his, and the words caught in the back of her throat. Heat swirled in her chest and rushed up to her cheeks. She'd never been this close to him.

If she were to lean forward just a few inches, her lips would touch his. And in that moment, it was all she could think about. What would he do if she kissed him?

Her heart pitter-pattered at the thought. She knew she should turn away, but her body refused to cooperate. It was then she noticed Colin's gaze dip down to her lips. Was he actually thinking of kissing her? The thought made her heart beat even faster.

But kissing Colin meant caring about Colin, and she wasn't prepared to do that. Every person she'd cared about in this life had left her—that included Colin. She wasn't prepared to be hurt again—especially if this was just something casual to him.

It took all of her self-restraint when she pulled away. His hands fell away from her shoulders. She wanted to walk away, but when she glanced down, she found Tater Tot's leash wrapped around her ankles.

"Looks like Tater Tot tripped you up. Here. Let me help you." He knelt down to guide Tater Tot back around to release the leash from her ankles.

The moment, however brief it had been, was over. She was surprised when a sense of disappointment washed over her. Did that mean she'd wanted him to kiss her? Oh, who was she trying to kid? Of course she wanted him to kiss her, but she just couldn't let it happen.

Chapter Nine

S HE ENJOYED HIS COMPANY.

The following day, Holly found herself thinking of Colin every time the shop grew quiet. She told herself she wasn't falling for him. They were just old friends. They'd shared a childhood next door to each other. Nothing more.

He'd grown into a mighty fine man. He was devastatingly handsome. He was thoughtful. And he was fun to be around. How was it that someone hadn't already snapped him up?

She'd enjoyed spending time with him. The truth was that she'd spent her free time alone since her grandmother passed on. These days she rarely hung out with her friends. The last time she saw Belle, they'd had coffee, and that was the day they'd first met Candi. These days the only people she spoke to were the customers in the shop.

It wasn't that she'd ended up in this position intentionally. At first, she'd needed alone time to process the loss of her grandmother. And then she'd gotten so caught up in settling the estate and keeping the shop open she hadn't had the time or the energy to socialize.

Maybe that was why she found herself looking forward to Colin's visits. And then there was that moment in the barn. Had he been thinking about kissing her? Or was her imagination working over-time?

When the front door jingled, Tater Tot started to bark. She shushed him. Lucky for her, he listened to her...at least, most times. Still, she had to deal with another customer. *Please, let them leave quickly.*

When she looked toward the door, there stood Belle with a bag in her hand. She lowered the hood of her coat. "I brought lunch." Then her gaze searched for the source of the barking. "Do you have a dog?"

"Uh, yeah. Well, kind of."

Belle approached her. "How do you kind of have a dog?"

"Arf-arf!"

"See for yourself." Holly released Tater Tot from his line. He barked as he raced around the counter.

She followed him. When he spotted Belle, he made a beeline toward her. He stopped in front of her and craned his neck to look up at her. He started to bark again.

Belle knelt down. "Hey, cutie. What's your name?"

"It's Tater Tot," Holly said.

"Wait. Is this one of the puppies that came to Kringle Falls with Odie?"

"Uh. Yeah."

Belle's smile broadened. "That's great. We can have puppy playdates." The excitement was evident in her voice. "We can include Candi with Tank. And then the puppies will be back together."

Tater Tot's tail wagged so fast his backend moved side to side. He inched forward, all the while sniffing the air. Belle held her hand out to him. They made fast friends.

"I don't know about the playdates," Holly said. "I won't have him much longer."

Belle looked at her with a wide-eyed stare. "Wait. What?"

"I'm just fostering him until Merry can find him an appropriate home. She had one, but there was an emergency, and they couldn't take him. So, we're just waiting for her to locate another family."

Belle looked down at Tater Tot, who was rubbing all over her, and then she looked back at Holly. "Please tell me you're going to keep him."

Holly shook her head. "I, uh... I can't."

"Sure, you can. Look how good he is. I'm guessing you two already have a routine."

As Belle was speaking, Holly continued to shake her head. She kept telling herself all of the reasons why it wouldn't work. But she was finding that as the days went by, she had less reasons not to keep Tater Tot. Still, she wasn't sure she was ready to open her home as well as her fragile heart.

Holly locked the door to the shop and put the "Out to Lunch" sign in the window. Then they moved to the little office in the back.

Belle took their salads out of the bag. "You wouldn't believe my day so far."

Holly got a couple of waters out of the little fridge next to the desk. "I don't know. You wouldn't believe my week."

Belle sat down and handed her a plastic fork and napkin. "Well, I got pulled over by the sheriff."

Holly nodded. "I heard. And I've been spending time with Colin."

"I heard that too."

"You did?"

"There's nothing that goes unnoticed in this small town. And the fact you're hanging out with one of the Bishop brothers—the one you had the biggest crush on—only made tongues wag faster."

Heat rushed to Holly's cheeks. Wanting to turn the attention away from herself, she said, "Why did you get pulled over this time? Please tell me you weren't speeding on those icy roads."

"No. Of course not. No. He pulled me over because my tail light was out."

"Oh. Well, that isn't so bad. Is it?"

Belle sighed. "Maybe if it was anyone but Parker Bishop. I swear that man sits around just waiting for me to make a mistake. This time it wasn't even my fault. How was I supposed to know my light was out?"

"You do have a point."

"So, tell me about you and Colin?" Belle's eyes lit up with interest.

"There's no Colin and me." She sighed. "He's been assisting me with Tater Tot. I don't know anything about dogs. So, he's been helping me figure things out."

"Things, huh?" There was a sing-song tone to her voice.

"Stop. It's not like that. You know he was never into me."

"So you say. But that was when you were kids. It's different now. You're both grown up, and there's no age barrier. What else have you two done together?"

Holly found herself opening up about him helping her bake cookies and sharing a couple of meals. And then the words came tumbling out about the almost kiss last night.

"So, now I don't know what to do," Holly said. "I don't know if I read things right last night or not."

"Uh-huh." Belle leaned back in her chair and was quiet for a moment. "Here's what I think you should do..."

What should he do?

All day long, Colin was thinking up reasons to go see Holly. So far, he hadn't come up with a legit reason to go knocking on her door. Still, he wasn't giving up.

He'd seen her surprise at all of the animals when she'd visited his place. She'd tried to hide her reaction, but he could tell she felt overwhelmed. It wasn't the first time it had happened. In the past, he'd excuse the reaction and assure himself that his girlfriend would get used to having all of the animals around.

At first, they would think the dogs, cats, and assorted pets were cute. But as time went by, they realized that most of those animals were staying permanently, and the ones that left for new homes would be replaced by other animals with equally heartbreaking stories. It was at this point that his relationships fizzled out.

He knew it would take a very special woman to fit into his world. He was starting to think she didn't exist. So, he'd given up on women and instead turned his full focus on helping animals.

His thoughts turned to that moment when he'd almost kissed Holly. He'd been so tempted. If she hadn't moved, he would have given into his desire and pressed his lips to hers.

Just the thought had his heart thumping. But kissing her would change their relationship. It would then include expectations and obligations. This is the point where all of his past relationships had started to go off the rails.

Maybe if he could keep things friendly, he could keep Holly in his life. Now that they'd renewed their friendship, he couldn't imagine his life without her in it.

He shoved aside the thoughts as he ducked out of the clinic after seeing his last patient. He didn't do any of his office work. He didn't hang around and speak to the staff like he normally did.

He planned to spend some time with his own animals while he worked to come up with even the flimsiest excuse to go see Holly. He tried to tell himself he wasn't falling for her, but that wasn't the truth. He was falling head over heels. It was scary and exhilarating at the same time. He'd never felt like this about a woman.

He knew he had to take his time with her. He didn't want to scare her off. And he knew she had old wounds when it came to letting down her guard with people. But he wasn't just anyone. He was one of her oldest friends. That had to count for something.

He raced upstairs to change into some casual clothes before wrestling with the dogs. He had to be careful they didn't get too rowdy in the house. He didn't want them getting hurt.

Knock-knock-knock.

The dogs barked as they ran for the door. "Thor! Spuds! Harley! Come." After a few more barks, they came back into the living room. "Sit." He had to tell them a couple more times.

Some more knocking drew his attention back to the front door. That was strange. He wasn't expecting anyone.

"Coming!" He got up off the floor and moved to the front door. He swung it open and blinked. "Holly, what are you doing here?"

She smiled at him, which made his heart thump. In one arm, she held Tater Tot in a little red and green plaid coat, and in her other hand was a pizza box. She held it out to him. "I brought dinner." Then her smile faltered. "Unless you've already eaten."

"I haven't." He pushed the door open wider. "Here. Come on in."

She stepped inside, and the three dogs rushed to the door. When the dogs barked, he told them to quiet. They listened to him as he closed the door.

He smiled as he led her to the kitchen. His smile faltered when he saw the stack of dirty dishes in the sink. And his unread mail scattered over the table. "Uh, sorry about the mess. I wasn't expecting company."

She sent him a reassuring smile. "Don't be sorry. It just makes you more human rather than some sort of super hero."

"Super hero?" He couldn't help but laugh. No one had ever called him that. He shook his head as he gathered himself. "I'm no super hero."

"That's not what a lot of pet parents say. I've heard them sing your praises all over town. You're always on call for emergencies. It's great how you always putting your patients first."

He didn't say anything. He didn't know what to say. All of the things she'd just said were the reasons that none of his romantic relationships had ever worked out in the past. He wondered if she'd still feel the same way if they were in a relationship, and his work interrupted their evenings together.

He washed his hands and then opened a cabinet. There were no clean plates. A super hero would definitely have clean dishes when the prettiest woman in the world brought him dinner.

"How's paper plates?" he asked.

"Sounds good to me."

While they ate pizza, the dogs, including Tater Tot, ate their dinners from a line of metal bowls along the wall under the window. Colin told her about his day, and then she told him about her day. It wasn't exciting. It wasn't earthshattering. And yet it was the best dinner conversation he'd ever shared with anyone. She could read him the weather forecast, and he'd hang on her every word.

Together, they cleaned up after dinner. There wasn't much to do since the dishes went in the garbage. It felt good to have someone to share the mundane, routine things with. And yet when he was with her, nothing felt mundane or routine. Being with Holly turned his black and white life into technicolor.

He glanced at the time on his smart watch. "I need to go out to the barn and feed the animals."

"Can I come with you? I'd like to see Cupcake and Jinx again."

"Uh, sure." No one had ever offered to help him feed the animals. "Let me just get a few things."

He grabbed a large plastic bowl. He opened the fridge and pulled open the crisper drawer. He took out some carrots and added them to the bowl. He also added a couple small zucchini, spinach, and kale.

When he turned around, he noticed Holly eyeing up the little bowl of Christmas candy that his mother had dropped off. "Go ahead and have some. In fact, you can have all of it. I'll never eat it."

"How about I help you out with one piece?" She perused the bowl before selecting a peppermint starlight mint.

He placed the bowl of vegetables on the counter. He retrieved a cutting board and then with a butcher knife, he chopped it all up and placed it back into the bowl.

"It looks like someone's going to have a yummy dinner," she said. "Is there anything I can do?"

"Yes, you can put on your coat. It's time to go." Once they were both dressed, he opened the door for her. "Come on."

They bundled up and headed out into the wintery evening. As they neared little barn, big snowflakes began to fall and form a halo atop her head. He told himself not to let himself get too caught up in this evening—in her unexpected presence. After all, this was just a friendly gesture. It wasn't like she was falling for him.

When they stepped into the barn, they were greeted with oinks and bleating. Colin was a little jealous because he rarely got such a boisterous welcome. Then again, he couldn't blame them because when Holly smiled, it was like the sun had come out from behind a cloud.

As they both made a fuss over Cupcake and Jinx, Holly asked some more questions about the animals and about their care. It was like she was truly interested in them and by extension she was interested in him. At least that was what he hoped.

In the end, he let her feed both the pig and the goat. She turned to him with a sun-shiny smile. "I think they like me."

The warmth of her smile infused him from the inside out. "I think you're right. If you keep fussing over them, they're going to get spoiled."

When she looked into his eyes, his heart thumped in his chest. He'd never had this strong of a reaction with another person. There was something special about Holly.

His fingers tingled with the urge to reach out to her. He longed to let his fingertips trace down over her rosy cheeks. And then he'd run his thumb over her plump bottom lip.

His heart beat faster. It was all he could do not to pull her into his arms and kiss her. He raised his gaze to meet hers.

"You're such a good guy," she said. "It's not surprising. You were the same way as a kid."

"And you were always the inquisitive one. You haven't changed much either. You're still so beautiful." It was only after the last words crossed his lips that he realized he'd vocalized his thoughts.

She glanced away as the color in her cheeks intensified. "You don't have to say that."

"I do. I mean it. You're the most beautiful woman I've ever known." He stepped closer to her.

She looked at him. His heart was pounding when he reached out to her. His fingers wrapped around her upper arms. All the while, he continued to drown in her blue-gray eyes.

When he drew her toward him, she followed his lead until she was standing right in front of him. This was it. This was the moment he'd been waiting for. His heart thumped so loud it echoed in his ears.

He hesitated for just a second, but when she leaned into him, he lowered his head. He claimed her lips with his own. In that moment, he couldn't remember why he'd waited so long to kiss her.

As her lips moved beneath his, the pounding of his heart drowned out the sounds of the animals. Her kiss was sweet and tasted like peppermint candy. He would never again taste peppermint without recalling this very special moment.

Her hands moved over his shoulders and wrapped around the back of his neck. If it were possible to make time stand still, he wanted that to happen now.

The final pieces of his life felt as though they'd fallen into place as he held her. But he didn't want to think about what that truly meant. There would be time for that later.

For now, he wanted to enjoy this moment. There was no need for it to take on a serious tone. Serious never worked out for him. It was best to keep things light.

And so, he let himself live in the moment. Her kiss was so much sweeter than he'd ever imagined. She was so much more than he'd imagined. He wanted to hold her like this forever...

Although, Cupcake and Jinx had other ideas. They didn't appear to like being forgotten. So, they started making a fuss. Holly sprang out of his arms. Her lips were rosy and begging to be kissed again.

She averted her gaze. "I think they need something."

He smiled. "They just want some more attention. It's hard for them in the winter because they spend most of their time inside. When springtime comes, they'll be out in the yard, visiting with all of the passersby."

"Do people stop and pet them?"

He nodded. "If they're close enough to the fence."

"I guess I'll have to make sure and walk by this spring."

"Or you could just be my guest."

The color rushed back to her cheeks. "Or that."

He might not be ready for anything serious, but he didn't regret kissing her. Not one little bit. In fact, he might do it again if given the opportunity.

CHAPTER TEN

H E COULDN'T STOP THINKING about her.

And that was the reason Colin had been avoiding Holly. He just needed some space to clear his head. Because kissing her couldn't happen again.

Still, he kept thinking of Holly. He pictured her with Tater Tot in her arms. She might not have figured everything out about the puppy's care, but she wouldn't stop until she knew what she needed to do to take care of the pup. He smiled as he recalled their past. She could be as stubborn as he was.

He was pretty certain Merry Kringle had given Holly the puppy with the intent of her adopting him. Merry was known to be a bit of a matchmaker. She wasn't particular about whom she paired up. It could be two humans or a human and an animal. She just wanted everyone to be happy and loved.

Merry must have been concerned about Holly now that she was all alone. Well, she did have parents...somewhere in this world. No one had seen them since Holly was a little girl. Holly might as well have been an orphan. It had been a good thing she had the most amazing grandmother.

His thoughts strayed to her apartment. She didn't have so much as one Christmas decoration up. Maybe she needed a little help finding her Christmas spirit.

With the thought in mind, he drove home. After fussing over the dogs and checking on Cupcake and Jinx, he headed to Holly's place. When he reached her building, he noticed someone exiting the soap company.

He was surprised to find the business still open. He didn't know why that should surprise him. After all, it was only going on five o'clock. He'd gotten out of work early because there were less appointments at this time of the year. People were busy and didn't have time for checkups. It was fine by him. The New Year would be here soon enough, and those patients would have his calendar full.

He headed toward the shop. He noticed a sign in the window with the hours. It closed at five. There were still a couple of customers meandering up and down the aisles. Holly was behind the counter. She glanced up when he walked in. Her eyes widened, and then she smiled.

While she checked out one of the two ladies, he looked around. He was impressed with the small gift baskets. They were eye-catching with big red bows. He was certain his mother would like them. He made a mental note to come back and pick up one for his mother.

He still had his father to shop for, but he was thinking about getting him a saltwater fishing rod. Now that his father was retired, he was looking into getting a boat. Colin was proud of himself for having a good idea.

But there was one more gift he had to figure out. He'd gotten together with his brothers to do secret Santa. They drew names at Thanksgiving. He'd pulled his youngest brother's name. He had no idea what to get Justin. He was still thinking it over.

"Sorry to keep you waiting." Holly joined him.

He heard a whine. Colin turned to find Tater Tot tethered to the checkout counter. The pup was pulling on the line, trying to follow Holly over to him.

Her gaze moved to Tater Tot. "I didn't know what else to do with him. I just couldn't leave him home alone. He cries every time I walk out of the room. I can't imagine what he'd do if he was left in the apartment all alone."

"As long as he was crated, he'd be safe and get used to it."

She sent him an *I-don't-believe-you* look. "Are you looking for a gift for a special someone?"

He cleared his throat. "No. No one special. But I was thinking of picking out one of your gift baskets for my mother. I think she'd like it."

A smile appeared on Holly's beautiful face. "Can I help you pick one out?"

"Uh... Maybe later. I want you—well, both of you—to come with me."

"I can't. The shop is still open."

He checked his smart watch. "According to the sign on the door, you closed eleven minutes ago, and there are no customers."

"Well, um... Where do you want to go?"

"It's a surprise." He sent her a reassuring smile.

She hesitated. "I don't know."

"Arf! Arf!"

He glanced over at the pup. "I think Tater Tot wants to go."

She rolled her eyes. "He would agree to anything that got him out of this shop."

"I see. Well, then let's go. Your carriage awaits."

She laughed. "My carriage, huh?" She peered out the window. "I don't see any carriage."

He sighed. "Fine. It's my pickup. But if you used your imagination, it could be a carriage."

She laughed some more, and it sounded wonderful to his ears. "I don't have that good of an imagination."

He feigned a pouty look. "Does that mean you won't come with me?"

"Arf! Arf!" Tater Tot kept pulling on his leash, trying to get loose.

Her gaze moved from Colin to Tater Tot and back again. "I shouldn't. I have a lot to do."

"But..."

She sighed. "But I suppose I have a little bit of time. Do you promise we won't be gone long?"

"I promise."

She eyed him up, as though trying to decide if she could trust him. Then she said, "If you want to get Tater Tot, I'll run in back and get my boots and coat."

"Sounds like a plan." He set off toward the pup, who went into a string of excited barks.

At least someone was happy to see him. He wondered if he'd ruined their friendship with the kiss the other day. He hoped not. He enjoyed every moment he'd spent with Holly.

Tater Tot jumped all over him as he worked to free his leash from the leg of the counter. When he finally picked up the pup, Tater licked Colin's face from forehead to chin and everywhere in between.

He carried Tater to the door. When the pup started to squirm, he said, "Calm down. Your momma will be here soon—"

"His what?"

He looked up in time to see Holly frowning at him. "You, uh, heard that?"

"Yes. And you're wrong." She crossed her arms as she continued to frown at him. "I'm not his mother. Not even close." She flipped off the light, pushed the door open, and stepped out into the winter evening. The cold breeze carried her soft voice back to him. "I no longer have any family. I'm alone. And that's the way it's going to remain."

Her words were like a punch in the gut. He felt her loneliness in that admission. He wanted to wrap his arms around her and assure her that she didn't have to be alone unless she wanted to be.

She didn't say anything further as she proceeded to lock the front door.

When she turned to go to the left, he said, "Wrong way. I'm parked over here."

Her head swung around. "Oh. Yeah."

He walked over and opened the passenger side door for her. Once she got in, he handed her the dog. After closing the door, he strode around the front of the pickup and got in the driver's side.

He started the engine and cranked up the heat. When he glanced over at Holly, she was staring straight ahead. "Holly, you forgot your seatbelt."

"Oh, yeah."

After she clicked her seatbelt into place, he put the pickup in gear and pulled out. They didn't have far to go. Kringle Falls wasn't that big. But they did have to go to the other side of town.

It was okay. They didn't have to talk. He could do silence. *Wait.* No, he couldn't. He enjoyed their conversations.

"So, the dogs are missing Tater Tot. They were wondering if he could come over for a play date."

She didn't say anything.

"I, uh, meant to stop by yesterday, but things were busy at the clinic. It's like the Kringle Falls furry population all had accidents. Let's see, there was a dog that ate two Christmas ornaments. Luckily, they weren't glass. Can you believe that? He's still under observation. We're hoping it'll pass, but we don't know."

"We had a cat that thinks it is Houdini. One moment the cat was on the exam table. The next moment, the cat had disappeared. We had to chase him throughout the office. At one point, we lost sight of him. The next thing you know, we find him sleeping on my desk chair." He chanced a quick glance at Holly, who was staring down at Tater Tot and petting him. "And then we found three newborn kittens abandoned by the door. Luckily a patient's parent stumbled upon them before they froze. They are now fed and warm."

"How do you do that?" she asked.

"Do what?" He put on the turn signal.

"Take care of animals that other people are willing to discard? Not exactly the kittens but the other animals that are injured and stuff."

He shrugged. "I guess I see what other people can't or aren't willing to see."

"And what's that?"

"That behind their growls and cowering is fear. I know that in their flaws, their strength and beauty shines through."

When he glanced over at Holly, her mouth gaped. It took her a moment to find her voice. "You are very special. All of the animals that pass through your life are very lucky to have known you."

He shook his head. "I don't deserve your kind words. I don't do anything special."

"But you do." She was quiet for a moment, as though searching for the right words. "You do more for them than some parents do for their own children."

Ouch. He didn't see that coming. Even when they were kids, she rarely mentioned her parents. He had no idea what he was supposed to say in response. And so, he chose not to say anything at all.

A couple minutes later, they'd arrived at their destination. He hoped this outing would lift Holly's spirits.

Holly looked around. "The Wagner Tree lot. Why did you bring us here?"

He turned off the engine before turning to her. "I thought that would be obvious. To get a Christmas tree."

She looked puzzled. "You already have a tree."

"Not for me. It's for you."

Her eyes lit up. Then she shook her head. "I don't think so. You've seen my place. It's not exactly ready for Christmas decorations."

"There's nothing wrong with your place."

She rolled her eyes. "You're just being kind."

"Don't worry about it. We'll find a tree to fit in the corner of the living room."

She shook her head. "No."

He turned in his seat until he was able to look into her eyes. "Would your grandmother want this for you? She loved the holidays. I remember when we were kids how she would decorate the front yard and the porch. Do you remember that giant snowman she had? And it wasn't one of the blow-up kind. It was solid plastic. That thing used to scare me."

Holly let out a laugh. "Me too."

He arched a brow. "Really?" When she nodded, he said, "I thought I was the only one. Do you still have it?"

"Are you kidding? It's one of the first things I got rid of when I cleaned out the garage. Would you believe some family bought it at the yard sale?"

"I hope they didn't have kids."

"Actually, they had two littles."

Colin groaned. "Those poor kids."

"I know."

He smiled at her. He loved being able to share these memories with her. "What do you say? Wanna get a tree?"

She sighed. "Okay. I'll do it for Gran. But I can't promise I'll be able to find the decorations."

"One problem at a time."

As he got out of the pickup, he realized she wasn't going to have much of a Christmas. Now that her grandmother was gone, she probably didn't feel that it mattered. But it did matter. She mattered. More than he was willing to admit.

She met him in front of the pickup. She carried Tater Tot. He noticed she kept petting the pup. She was getting attached. He could see it, but he didn't know if she had realized it yet. He wasn't going to mention it. He didn't want her defenses to go up. He knew how much puppy love could help heal broken hearts. He'd seen the transformation time and time again.

Holly didn't say it, but he could see the loss of her grandmother had left her broken. He felt guilty for being so caught up in his own life that he hadn't realized she needed a friend—a good friend.

They entered the busy tree lot. Strings of lights were strung high in the air. And on the speakers "We Wish You a Merry Christmas" played. There were big pine trees and small ones. There were fat ones and skinny ones. Blue spruce and scotch pines. There were firs and so many more. And all were dusted with a fresh coating of snow.

"What do you think?" He walked next to her, taking in the many Christmas trees.

"I don't know. There are so many."

Then he had an idea to get this process started. "What sort of tree did you and your grandmother get?"

"She had an artificial that we put up every year."

"Oh." He hadn't foreseen that answer. "Do you want to put that up instead?"

She shook her head. "It sold at the yard sale."

"Oh." He realized that he kept saying the same thing, but she kept surprising him with her answers. He cleared his throat and tried again. "Do you have a particular type of tree in mind?"

"I don't know." She looked around. "Maybe it should be something small?"

"Why?" He didn't care, but he was curious about her line of thought.

"I don't know." She shrugged. "That way I can tuck it away in a corner where it's out of the way."

He thought about trying to convince her that a big, bold tree would light up the room, but he ultimately changed his mind. As long as she picked out a tree, even if it was a Charlie Brown tree, he'd be happy. After all, he was always telling his patients' parents to take recovery slowly, one step at a time.

When she didn't pick out a tree or even show any interest in any of the trees, he took a more active role. He purposely picked out an imperfect tree. "What about this one?"

She walked over to the tree that he gestured toward. She walked the whole way around it. "Not this one."

"Why?"

Her nose crinkled up. "Didn't you see the big holes between the branches? There's one on this side and one on the other side."

Oh, yes, he'd seen them. He just wanted to spark some involvement from her.

When they walked a little bit, he said, "Here's a tree. And it's short."

She looked at it, and her head tilted to the left side. "It's crooked. The trunk leans to the left."

"Good thing you caught it." He hid a little smile.

"You're obviously not good at this. So..." She walked over to a tree, looked at it, and then moved on to another tree. "What about this one?"

He tried to hide his surprise that she pointed out a blue spruce that was just north of six feet. He resisted the urge to smile. Instead, he strolled over to look at it.

"I don't know..." He liked the tree, but he didn't want to look too enthusiastic, because he didn't want her to change her mind.

She frowned at him. "What don't you know about? The tree is perfect."

"Isn't that a hole?" He pointed to a random place on the tree. There wasn't a hole, but he knew the more he was in opposition to it, the more she would fight for the tree.

She walked over and squinted at the tree. "What hole? There isn't one."

"Are you sure?"

"Yes. I'm positive. This is the tree."

As though to finalize the decision, Tater Tot barked.

"I guess that's two against one," Colin said. "You win. We'll get this one."

Before she had a chance to change her mind, he picked up the tree and carried it over to pay one of the attendants. Holly insisted on paying. On the way to his pickup, he finally let the smile emerge.

"What are you smiling about?" she asked.

"Nothing. Absolutely nothing." He placed the tree in the back of the pickup. It didn't completely fit, so a little bit hung over the tailgate.

"Well, don't look so pleased with yourself. Now you have to help me decorate the tree."

"I do, huh?"

"Yes. It's non-negotiable."

They got into the pickup and headed back to her place. Tater Tot was getting wiggly. She let him loose, and the next thing Colin knew, Tater Tot stood up against his shoulder and licked his cheek.

Colin slowed the pickup at a stop sign. "What kind of decorations are you thinking for the tree?"

"I don't know. I guess the only decorations I have. If we can find them."

He stepped on the accelerator. Her apartment was just a few buildings up the road. "We'll find them..."

"What in the world?" Surprise rang out in her voice.

"What's wrong?"

"All of the lights are on in my place. I know I turned them off and locked up when we went to leave. Colin, I think someone broke in?"

He slowed down and stared up at the lights glowing in the windows. "But this is Kringle Falls. Nothing ever happens here." He watched as one by one the lights were turned off. "Don't worry. It'll be okay."

"No, it won't."

CHAPTER ELEVEN

A BREAK-IN?

Things like this didn't happen in Kringle Falls. At least it didn't used to happen.

Colin couldn't help but think of Belle Sinclair's dog being stolen right out of her house. Was this some sort of crime wave breaking out in his hometown? The thought left an uneasy feeling in the pit of his stomach.

He glanced over to see Holly's hand already on the door handle. He needed to stop her, but he couldn't do that and keep the pickup from sliding out of control on the icy roadway.

"Holly, you can't go rushing in there. We need to call the sheriff." Colin pulled the pickup to the side of the road.

"You call." With Tater Tot tucked under her arm, she opened the door before the truck was stopped.

"Holly! Wait!" He tramped the brake. The pickup slid across the sheet of ice on the road.

Without bothering to park, he threw the pickup into Park and jumping out. By then, Holly was already across the street. What did she think she was going to do?

He rushed to catch up to her. His finger had barely grazed her upper arm when the door to her apartment opened. In the glow from the light next to the doorway, he was able to make out a man and a woman. They didn't appear to have anything in their arms. He supposed that should be a relief.

Holly came to a halt on the sidewalk. Tater Tot started to bark while Holly remained silent. Was she afraid? Perhaps. It wasn't every day you find strangers walking out of your home.

He stepped past her. "You need to stop right there." He pulled his phone from his pocket. "I'm calling the sheriff."

"Don't." Holly's voice was soft but firm as she stepped up beside him.

"Holly, do you recognize us?" The woman wore a too-bright smile.

He turned to Holly. He wondered if she knew them, because he sure didn't. In fact, he'd be willing to swear that he'd never seen them before.

He still had his phone in his hand. He was ready to call his big brother Parker, who was the town's sheriff. His gaze moved between Holly and the people claiming to know Holly.

After a few awkward moments passed, Holly said, "You look like your pictures. What are you doing here?"

Pictures? Wait. Were these her parents? His gaze moved back and forth between Holly and those people.

The woman stepped toward Holly. Tater Tot growled.

Colin instinctively took a sidestep, as though to stop these people if they got too close to Holly. The woman's eyes lifted to meet his. Her displeasure with his interference was obvious on her thin face.

Her face was covered with deep lines, as though she'd lived a tough life. And when she smiled once more at Holly, the smile didn't look natural. It was as though she weren't used to smiling, and so her face looked as awkward as she must have felt.

"I just want to talk to my daughter." Her unspoken intention was to tell him to get out of her way.

He crossed his arms. He wasn't budging. "You can talk from there. She isn't hard of hearing."

The woman's friendly mask slipped, and a scowl came over her face. Her eyes were filled with anger. But in a blink, she resumed her fake smile. "Holly, can we go inside? It's cold out here."

"I'm good here." Holly's voice didn't sound like her. It was deeper than normal, and there was a firmness to it. "What are you doing here?"

The man stepped forward with a frown on his face. "That's no way to speak to your mother. After all, we came all of this way to see you."

Holly's voice was matter-of-fact. "You're six months too late for Gran's funeral."

While Holly's voice was devoid of emotion, her eyes were telling a different story. Colin wasn't sure if she was in shock or if she was afraid of them. Either way, he was there for her. Whatever she wanted, he would make sure it happened.

"Uh… We meant to make it," her mother said.

"But we had a business opportunity present itself, and we couldn't say no." Her father lifted his chin, as though their excuse couldn't be challenged.

"How did you get in my apartment?" Holly's gaze shifted between her mother and father.

Her mother sighed. "We went to the house first. Imagine out surprise when we learned that you sold it without saying anything to us."

"And imagine my surprise when you didn't show up for Gran's funeral. Oh, wait. I wasn't surprised."

The woman fidgeted with her purse strap. "Anyway, this was our apartment before it was yours." She pulled out a keyring from her purse and showed Holly a key. "See."

Holly held out her palm. "Give it to me."

"What?" Her mother frowned. "No. I won't."

Holly stepped up to the woman as Tater Tot resumed growling at her parents. "Give me the key. Now."

There was a strained moment before the woman yanked the key off the ring and handed it over. Holly took it and stuffed it into her pocket.

"What are you doing here now?" There was absolutely no friendliness in Holly's voice.

"Well, honey"—her mother's voice took on a sugary-sweet tone—"it was my mother who died. We wanted to come back and take care of things."

"She died six months ago." Holly's expression was unreadable.

"We explained that, honey." Her mother took a step forward. When Holly took a step back, her mother said, "It's all in the past. We're here now. Let's go upstairs so we can settle in. It was a long trip."

Holly shook her head. "You aren't staying here."

"Yes, we are." Her father stepped forward. "I don't understand this hostility. I thought you'd be happy to see us. Now let's go upstairs."

"No." Holly walked through the snow to get around them. She gave her parents a wide berth.

Colin followed her. When she came to a stop in front of the door to her apartment, she glanced over at him. The surprise shone in her eyes. If she thought he was leaving her alone with these two, she couldn't be more wrong.

Her parents turned to her. Their lips were pressed into firm lines, as if they were holding back their words of frustration because Holly wasn't falling into their arms.

"Where do you expect us to stay?" her father asked.

"I don't know." Holly sighed, as though she were tired of dealing with them. "That's not my problem."

Her mother stepped forward, but when she saw the formidable look on her daughter's face, she stopped. "I can't believe you sold the homeplace and moved here. You should have consulted me before doing any of this."

Holly glared at the woman. "If you cared, you would have been here."

"We had business to take care of."

Holly shook her head. "I'm not talking about when Gran died. You should have been here years ago. Things have changed."

"Holly, you're just tired. Get some rest. We can talk in the morning." Her mother sent her a tentative smile.

When the woman stepped forward with her arms outstretched, Holly held up her palm. "Stop."

It was just one word, but it was enough to get her mother to do exactly that.

Holly turned and entered the building. Her parents hesitated on the sidewalk, as though considering following her inside. Colin couldn't think of a worse idea.

"You should go now." He wanted to tell them to keep going, straight out of town, but he resisted the urge.

Perhaps her mother was right. In the morning, Holly might decide to let her only family back into her life. He couldn't see that happening, but stranger things were known to happen. Either way, it was Holly's decision. And whatever she decided, he would have her back.

They are back.

They are back.

Holly's heart was pounding as her breath came in rapid succession. She rushed up the stairs to her apartment. She felt as though her life had been blown up again. And she realized that was not the normal response when one saw their parents. Nothing about her life had been "normal."

Tears of frustration stung the backs of her eyes. She blinked repeatedly. She refused to give in to them. Her parents weren't deserving of her tears. The truth was that she'd already shed enough over them.

What were her parents doing there? And why were they in her apartment? She looked around but didn't see anything disturbed. That was a relief.

She stepped into the kitchen and placed Tater Tot on the floor. He raced to the living room window and stared out into the darkness as he barked. It was as if he were warning her parents to stay away.

When he noticed her looking at him, he ran over to her. Tater jumped up, putting his paws against her thigh. She was tempted to pick him up and cuddle him. There was something about having his tiny body in her arms that always made her feel better.

And that was when she knew what she needed to do. She reached for her phone and called Merry. The phone rang once, twice...

By the fifth ring, it switched over to voicemail. "Merry, this is Holly. I was checking in to see if you have found Tater Tot a new home. It's been a few days now. Anyway, please give me a call back and let me know. Bye."

She slipped the phone back into her pocket. She still couldn't figure out what her parents were doing in Kringle Falls. She didn't believe they were there just to visit with her. They could have seen her a million different times throughout her life, but they never had time. What made this different?

All of a sudden there were hands on her upper arms. She jumped.

"Relax." Colin's voice was soft and close to her ear. "They're gone."

She leaned back against him. She let out a pent-up breath. "I can't believe they're in Kringle Falls."

"Are you okay?" His arms wrapped around her mid-section. "Can I do anything?"

She shook her head. "I'm fine." She didn't feel fine. Her heart had longed to jump into her mother's arms, while her mind warned her that her parents always had an agenda that centered around themselves. "I, uh..." She glanced around. "I need to..."

"Find the Christmas decorations," he said.

She moved out of his embrace. "I'm not in a Christmas mood."

"Don't let them ruin the evening. We were having some fun. And there's a tree in my pickup just waiting for some lights and ornaments."

She didn't want to trim a tree, but Colin had gone out of his way to bring some Christmas cheer into her life. She didn't have the heart to turn him down. And so, she'd fake a bit of holiday spirit and decorate the tree for Colin's sake.

Pushing thoughts of her parents to the back of her mind, she said, "Okay. But I can't promise we'll find the ornaments." Her gaze moved to the stacks of boxes she hadn't unpacked yet. "If I still have them, they are in there. Somewhere."

"How about you start looking while I get the tree?"

"Okay."

Tater Tot ran over to her side and sat down. Holly set to work, opening the boxes. She'd been putting off this task. She just wasn't ready to see the stuff that reminded her of her loving grandmother. A pang of grief stabbed at her heart.

Holly wondered what her grandmother would think of her parents' arrival. Gran never minced words. She'd probably have told them that they were too late and slammed the door in their faces.

Maybe that was what she should have done. Instead, she'd left the door cracked open. Would her parents be back the next day? And if they were, what would she say to them?

She moved a box from the top of the stack. She placed it on the floor and ripped off the packing tape. She didn't know what was inside. Halfway through the moving process, she'd run out of time and patience. This box was unmarked.

She opened the flaps and stared inside at nothing more than bubble wrap. Something told her this was not the box with Christmas ornaments. But that didn't stop her from picking up the first item and unwrapping it.

It was a framed picture of her and her grandmother. It had been taken at Holly's high school graduation. A few months ago, it would have made her cry, but on this day, she found herself smiling through the pain.

"Oh, Gran. I wish you were still here..."

"What did you say?"

She spun around to see Colin standing there. "Uh, nothing. I didn't find the decorations yet."

"Don't worry. We'll find them, but first, can you help me get the tree up the stairs?"

"Uh, sure." She started for the stairs.

The only thing was that with all of the boxes in the room, there wasn't much standing room. Her foot struck a box. She lost her balance. She fell into Colin. His arms wrapped around her until she regained her balance.

When she tilted her chin upward to thank him, their gazes met and held a moment longer than necessary. Thoughts of her parents and the missing ornaments slipped to the back of her mind. There was something about the intensity of his gaze that drew her in.

Her tattered heart beat with renewed life. There was something about being around Colin that had her wishing for things that she knew were out of reach.

She felt her body leaning against his muscled chest. At the same time, his gaze lowered to her lips. He was going to kiss her again. And she was going to let him.

"*Arf! Arf!*" Tater Tot ran and jumped on her leg.

And the moment was over as quickly as it had started. Holly glanced down at the pup and petted his head. Then she turned and headed for the stairs.

What was she doing wanting Colin to kiss her? She of all people knew the risk of letting herself care about someone else. It was always a gamble. And the odds were against her.

This whole evening felt as if it were spinning out of control. Since her grandmother died, she'd been working so hard to get her life under control. Little by little she worked toward that goal.

It started with selling her childhood home in order to settle her grandmother's medical bills and then creating herself a new home. But now with her parents in town and Colin looking at her like he wanted to kiss her again, she felt that control slipping from her grasp.

To her relief, they had an easy time of getting the tree up the stairs. With Tater Tot yapping at them the whole time, they made it to the living room without incident. Colin propped the tree up in the corner.

Holly slipped off Colin's coat and hung it on the back of the kitchen chair. Then she set to work finding the ornaments. She was determined to find them in short order.

She knew Colin wouldn't leave until they decorated the tree. And she just needed some alone time to decompress and figure out what her parents' presence meant.

It was the fourth box she opened that held the old ornaments. It was a huge box and so heavy she couldn't lift it. So she dragged it across the floor.

When she spotted her grandmother's favorite ornaments, she was immediately hit with memories of Christmases gone by. She lifted one of the snowmen ornaments and dangled it from her fingertip. The glitter made the snowman sparkle.

She thought of her grandmother fussing over the tree, wanting to get the ornaments in just the right place. The memory brought a smile to her face. Oh, how she missed Gran. She could use her advice now that Roger and Billie Jean were back in town.

"What are you thinking about?" Colin's voice drew her back to the present.

"Oh, I was just thinking about Gran. She loved this time of the year."

"So, she would be happy that you got a tree."

"Yes, she would." If it weren't for Colin, she wouldn't be putting up the tree. And she wouldn't have had these happy memories to warm her heart. "Thank you."

His brows rose. "For what?"

"For making me go get a tree and for digging through these ornaments. It reminded me of Gran." Barely more than whisper, she said, "I miss her so much."

"I know you do." He put an arm over her shoulders and pulled her close. "She would want you to be happy."

"I wish I could ask her what to do about my parents. I can't believe they're here."

He squeezed her shoulders tighter. "I know it's not the Christmas you want, but we can still make it fun."

She moved to the box of decorations. "Then you better get busy."

"Me? I thought this was a joint endeavor."

"I seem to recall that it was your idea."

"But it's for us to do together. Come on." He carried the decorations to the living room, where Tater Tot was stretched out on the couch. He lifted his head, yawned, and then went back to sleep. "I don't think he's going to be very much help."

Holly checked the time. "That's because it's almost his bedtime."

"Bedtime?"

Holly nodded. "It's lights out at nine. Don't your dogs have a bedtime?"

He laughed. "No. No, they don't."

She shrugged. "To each their own."

When he laughed some more, she said, "Stop laughing. I'm just trying to be a good foster mom."

He stopped laughing and smiled at her. "You're being the best foster mom. Tater Tot is a very lucky fellow." Colin pulled everything out of the box. "Here it is."

He held up the tree stand. The green and red stand was nailed to a two-by-two piece of wood. No wonder the box was so heavy.

He turned to her. "Can you help me?"

"Uh... Sure. What do you want me to do?"

"Well, you can hold the tree upright, or you can get down on the floor and tighten the stand to hold the tree. It's your choice."

So, either her arms got poked by pine needles or she lay on the floor and hoped the needles didn't fall all over her. Not great choices. "I think I'll hold up the tree."

He smiled at her. "Okay. Let's get it in the stand."

For the next half hour, they fussed over the tree. It was a lot harder to get the tree straight than she would have imagined.

It was nice to have someone there to do this with. She couldn't see herself doing it alone. Eventually, Tater Tot got up off the couch to inspect their work.

And when Colin got down on the floor, the pup was all over him. Tater Tot stood on Colin's chest and licked his face. Holly found herself laughing because it was so ridiculous. She even snapped a couple of pictures, contrary to Colin's complaints.

Once Tater moved to a different spot under the tree, Colin was able to tighten the six bolts that held the tree in place. He'd just tightened the last bolt when a beeping started.

Holly frowned as she tried to figure out what was going off. "Can I let go? I need to find out what is beeping."

"You can let go, but the beeping is me." He got to his feet. "Sorry. I have to go. Cupcake needs her medicine."

"Oh. Yes. Sure. I didn't mean to keep you." And then she realized she should have offered to feed him. "I owe you dinner."

His eyes widened. "I accept. I'll see you tomorrow."

That wasn't exactly what she had in mind. It was more of something to say than an actual invitation. But before she could say anything else, Colin was gone.

She was left with thoughts of the nice evening that had been ruined by the unexpected appearance of her parents. What were they doing in Kringle Falls? Her grandmother swore her parents hated this town. So, what had changed their minds?

CHAPTER TWELVE

IT HADN'T BEEN A restful night.

Saturday morning, Holly struggled not to yawn in front of the customers. She'd grabbed her largest insulated cup from the cabinet, and she'd filled it with coffee, milk, and sugar. She'd sipped on it throughout the morning.

Even though she'd tossed and turned much of the night, she still hadn't come up with the reason her parents had picked this particular moment to come back to town. She hadn't heard from them at all that morning. Was it wrong of her to just want them to go away? Maybe they realized they'd made a mistake and headed off to deal with their "business."

She pushed away the unwanted thoughts, and in their place, Colin's image formed in her mind. A smile tugged at the corners of her lips. In her mind, she visualized Colin walking through the doorway of the soap company. Her smile broadened. If only...

Her gaze shifted to Tater Tot, who was curled up in the bed Holly had made for him behind the counter. She noticed he'd dragged his blue blanket out of the bed, so she knelt down to pick it up. "You're going to get cold."

She petted Tater Tot before she began to tuck the blanket around the pup. Just then the door jingled.

"*Arf! Arf-arf!*"

"Shh... It's okay."

"*Arf! Arf!*"

"Tater, quiet." When the dog paused, she said, "Welcome to the Kringle Soap Co. I'll be right with you." She finished positioning the little blanket around Tater Tot. She straightened. "Merry, it's good to see you." But was it really? She glanced down at Tater Tot before her gaze returned to Merry. "Are you here to take Tater Tot?"

"I'm afraid not. The family I had in mind are moving for work, and it's not a good time for them to adopt a dog."

Holly nodded. "I can understand. Moving is hard enough without taking a new pet."

"Then you'd be okay with him staying with you for a bit longer?"

She glanced down at Tater Tot. "I think we can manage."

Merry hesitated. "Are you sure?"

Holly looked down at Tater Tot as he chewed on his bone. He was a lot of work, and she did have to get out of bed an hour earlier to make sure Tater was taken outside, fed, and played with before they made their way downstairs to open up the shop.

And yet she knew what it was like to be abandoned and to feel unwanted. She didn't want that for Tater Tot. She would keep him until an appropriate and loving home was found for him.

"Yes." Her voice was firm. "We've got this." She glanced down at the pup, who looked up at her. "Huh, Tater?"

"Arf! Arf-arf!"

Merry smiled. "It sounds like he agrees."

Holly knelt down and released the line she'd rigged to keep Tater Tot from wandering off. Before she could hook his leash, he ran off. For a little guy with short legs, he was very fast.

"Tater Tot, come back."

He kept moving and turned the corner before she could catch him. She moved out from behind the counter and came to a stop next to Merry. She knew from experience that chasing after him would only make him run faster. He thought it was a game, and there was nothing she could say that would convince him it wasn't.

The shop was empty, so she let him nose his way around it. She knew that sooner or later, he would make his way back to her. He always did.

Merry's gaze followed the puppy. "He seems very happy."

Holly nodded. "It was a rough start, but we're starting to figure each other out."

Just then Tater Tot made his way over to her. She knelt down and picked him up. She snuggled him. In return, Tater Tot gave her a puppy smooch on the cheek.

"I'm glad to see things are going well. I need to be going." Merry petted the pup before heading for the door. "I'll be in contact as soon as I find the right home for him." And then she was gone.

Holly looked at Tater. "What do you think? Should we close for lunch? I can take you outside, and then we can get something to eat."

She stepped behind the counter to grab her phone and bag. *Jingle-jingle.* She looked toward the front door. In walked Billie Jean.

Holly couldn't bring herself to call them Mom and Dad. On the rare times that she'd mentioned them to her grandmother, she'd called them Billie Jean and Roger. She always thought the names *Mom* and *Dad* were earned through a steady loving presence. Her parents didn't provide her with any of those things. The best thing that had happened to her was ending up with her grandmother.

Compared to the old photos Holly had found amongst her grandmother's belongings, Billie Jean had aged a lot. There were deep lines etched around her eyes and her mouth. Her skin was tan, but it had a leathery appearance, as though she'd spent a lot of time in the sun. And there were little lines framing her mouth, as though she'd spent a lifetime smoking.

When her mother's gaze met hers, Billie Jean smiled. The action didn't look as though it came natural to her. Was it that her mother didn't smile often? Or was this whole appearance in Kringle Falls some sort of show? Or was it a little of both?

"Hello, dear." Again, the endearment sounded hollow coming from her mother. Billie Jean's gaze moved to the dog in Holly's arms. "What are you doing with that, um..."

"Puppy." Roger stepped forward. The smile on his face didn't quite reach his eyes. He reached out to pet Tater Tot.

The pup started to growl. His little body went stiff in her arms. Holly took a step back.

The smile fell from Roger's face. His hand lowered. "Not a very friendly thing, is he?"

Tater Tot continued to stare at Holly's parents as a low growl rumbled from him. Holly didn't even know he knew how to growl. He'd only ever been sweet and loving toward her.

She needed to get this meeting over with as quickly as possible. It was impossible to deal with them on a familial level, so she went with something natural for her.

"How may I help you?" She noticed how her words made Billie Jean's eyes momentarily widen.

Roger cleared his throat. "We came to take you to lunch."

"I, uh..." She hadn't been expecting that. The thought of sitting at a table with them for what? A half hour? Maybe an hour? And having to conjure up things to talk about sounded like a special kind of torture.

There was a part of her that had been waiting her entire life for a moment like this. As a child, she'd wished for this every Christmas. She'd wished for it upon a falling star. She'd even tried to make a deal with God, but she didn't think he'd been listening.

After years of yearning, was she ready to just turn her back on them? Now, they were actually making an attempt to have some sort of relationship with her. It had to mean something, right?

Still, the protective wall she kept around her heart prompted her to say, "I can't. The shop...I have the shop to run."

Her mother stepped up next to her father. "But you have to eat, right?"

"I, uh..." Her mind searched for another excuse and failed.

"Come on," Roger said. "You can close for lunch. We'll be back in no time."

"I, uh..." She realized she was having trouble stringing together words in order to form actual sentences. "I need to take care of Tater Tot."

"It won't take long, will it?" Billie Jean asked.

"It's okay. Do what you need to do," Roger said. "We have time."

"I'll be back." Holly put the sign on the door that read: *Out to lunch.*

She rushed over to the apartment. She put on Tater Tot's little boots followed by his coat. She took him out, and as though sensing something was amiss, he was unusually fast at doing his business. She fed him lunch and then put him into his crate.

When he looked at her with his big, sad puppy eyes, she said, "I'm sorry. I won't be gone long."

And then she put on her coat. She wondered if she was making the right decision. After all, these were the people who missed her entire childhood. They didn't make it to her kindergarten graduation. They were nowhere to be seen for her sixth grade or high school graduation. They didn't even send flowers when her grandmother died. So, why was she doing this?

She supposed there was still that little girl inside of her who was hoping for a happy ending—who wanted to believe her parents were sorry and regretted missing out on her childhood. Was this her long ago Christmas wish coming true?

~elle~

He was worried about her.

Colin's last thought the night before had been of Holly. And she'd once again filled his thoughts when he'd awakened. They'd had such fun tree shopping. He'd finally gotten her to unwind. And then they'd returned to her place, only for her to be blindsided by her parents.

He took an instant dislike to them, which was unusual for him. Usually, he was good about giving people space and time to show their true colors. He didn't know if it was that they'd abandoned their daughter. Or maybe it was hearing Holly as a kid wondering what was wrong with her that her own parents didn't want her.

Then again, it could have been the way they'd barged into Holly's life. What were they doing in her apartment? Were they hunting for something in particular?

And then for them to expect Holly to be grateful to see them. If it were up to him, he would have told them to go back where they came from. But none of this was up to him.

With it being the weekend, the clinic was closed. He'd planned to swing by the soap company to see how Holly was doing, but before he made it out the door, his phone had rung. There had been an accident. It happened in the winter with the ice on the roads.

This time it was a dog struck by a car. He'd hit the ground running. He'd called his vet tech and met the very upset dog parents at the office. Since there wasn't an animal hospital close by, he was always on call.

Thankfully, the injury wasn't life-threatening. As they worked to set the dog's fractured leg, two more patients came in. He wanted to turn them away and go check on Holly, but he couldn't do that. Instead, he stayed and treated them.

It was nearing lunchtime by the time he got out of the clinic. He headed for the door, when it swung open and in strolled his brother Michael along with his puppy, Tank. Once inside, Tank did the full body shake that started at his head and ended with his fluffy tail. Pieces of snow and ice flung everywhere.

"Hey, Colin, I saw the lights on." Michael approached him. "Did you have an emergency?"

Colin nodded. "One emergency led to three of them. Now I'm trying to get out of here before someone else sees that the lights are on and stops in." His gaze moved to Tank. The dog looked like he was doing well after his adventure the other day. "Is everything all right with Tank?"

"Yeah. I wish I could say the same for Belle's dog."

"Has there been any news?"

Michael gave a quick shake of his head. "I've been stopping in every chance I get. The case just keeps getting stranger."

"If there's anything I can do, just let me know."

"Actually, I was wondering if you were going to the party tonight." When Colin sent him a confused look, Michael said, "You know, the Kringles' Christmas party."

"Oh. Right. Well, I don't know." He didn't normally go. But he liked the thought of taking Holly. *As friends only.*

"I was planning to take Candi. It'll be her first Christmas in Kringle Falls, and I don't want her to miss out on any of the traditions, since she loves the holidays so much. But obviously Parker won't be there. And Justin never goes."

"And you want me to go so you have someone to talk to?"

Michael nodded. "So, what do you say?"

"Mom and Dad will be there. They're always there."

"I know but it'd be great to have one of my brothers around."

He thought about Holly. He'd had a hard time talking her into going to get a Christmas tree. He had serious doubts about talking her into going to a big holiday party, but then he recalled her baking cookies for the party. "I don't know. I wouldn't count on me being there."

"But you could take Holly."

Colin arched a brow. How much did his brother know? "What are you talking about?"

Michael sighed and rolled his eyes. "You surely didn't think it had gone unnoticed that you've been spending a lot of time with her."

"I was just trying to help her with the dog she's fostering."

"Really?" Michael's eyes shone with amusement as he struggled not to smile. "How does visiting the Christmas tree lot help the dog?"

Colin glared at his brother. "I was being nice."

"Uh-huh. And I remember the huge crush she had on you when we were kids. Maybe she wasn't the only one with a crush. Huh?"

"Michael, stop. I have to go." He moved past his brother and headed for the door, where he paused and called over his shoulder, "Turn off the lights and lock up when you leave."

As he stepped outside, he heard his brother's laughter. Colin's back teeth ground together. It was so hard to do anything in a small town with a person of the opposite sex without people jumping to all of the wrong conclusions.

He climbed into his pickup and pulled out of the parking lot. Holly's place was across town. He glanced at the clock on the dash. It was after noon now. His brother had made him late.

He pressed a little heavier on the accelerator. He thought of calling her, but if she was already headed to lunch with friends or something like that, he didn't want to disturb her.

When he reached her block, he slowed down as he searched for a parking spot. But as his gaze swept the roadway side to side, he spotted Holly exiting the shop. He was about to roll down his window and offer her a ride to lunch, but then he noticed she wasn't alone.

Flanked on either side of her were her parents. He didn't know what to think. Then he saw Holly nodding her head and talking to them as they turned in the opposite direction of him. He wasn't sure what to do. He wanted to turn around and drive away, but that was impossible between the parked cars and the snow banks.

Instead, he pressed on the accelerator. Maybe she would be so busy talking to her long-lost relatives she wouldn't notice him drive by. He kept his gaze focused forward and kept going.

It was for the best. At least that was what he wanted to believe. Because he knew that if he had been there when her parents arrived, he would have done his best to keep Holly away from them.

He knew as sure as he was driving down the street that they were going to disappoint Holly again. He found it surprising Holly would let them into her life after their painful history. Then again, maybe it wasn't so surprising.

Holly didn't say how much she missed her grandmother, but it was in the pained look in her eyes. It was in the way she refused to unpack the boxes at the apartment. It was in the way she kept the soap company running just the way her grandmother would have done.

He just hoped that Holly knew what she was doing where her parents were concerned. He didn't want her getting hurt...again. Those people left a trail of devastation. At least they used to... Something told him that hadn't changed.

CHAPTER THIRTEEN

THE PEPPERMINT COURTYARD.

Really?

Holly was surprised this was where her parents wanted to have lunch, instead of the Kringle Cup Café. The Peppermint Courtyard was the fanciest dining in town. It didn't have a dress code or anything, but it was definitely a step up from the other places. This was the place that she dreamed about one day having dinner with Colin.

She glanced down at her blue jeans and white sweater. She felt underdressed. She looked around at the other patrons in their dress clothes. She didn't recognize many of them. The others must be tourists.

She glanced across the table at Billie Jean. Her brown hair was streaked with white. And even though she'd applied makeup, her face showed lines from, as her grandmother would say, hard living. When she held up the menu, Holly could see her nails were chewed to the quick.

Sympathy welled up in Holly, but she stamped it down. After all, these were the people who had abandoned her as a baby and only stopped back twice in her life. And then it struck her that this was only the third time she'd seen her parents since she was a baby. The third time. The thought landed like a rock in her stomach. She lost her appetite.

"What are you going to have, sweetie?" Roger asked.

Holly assumed he was speaking to Billie Jean, so she didn't say anything as she continued to stare down at the menu without seeing any of the words.

"Holly, did you hear me?" It was Roger's voice again.

She lowered the menu and looked at him. "Uh, sorry. What?"

He frowned at her with a look that said how-dare-you-not-hang-on-my-every-word. When Billie Jean elbowed him, he smiled. "I wanted to know what you're going to order."

"Oh. I don't know." Her gaze moved back to the menu and the prices. *Wow!* This place wasn't cheap. No wonder her grandmother never wanted to eat there.

"Well, I'm going to have the seared salmon with a side of couscous." Billie Jean set aside the menu.

"I'm having a New York Strip steak." Roger placed his menu on top of Billie Jean's.

Another *wow* spun through her mind. They certainly eat fancy for lunch. She usually just had a salad or burger. There were no burgers on the menu. So, she checked out the salads.

These salads were not your run-of-the-mill salads. They had a seared salmon with avocado. Another salad had Maine lobster. And the prices definitely matched the fancy salads. She didn't have the money to splurge on a salad, but her parents were here, so this made it a special occasion.

Her gaze landed on the last salad listed. It was a cobb salad with sliced tenderloin. It was the cheapest on the menu so that was the one she picked. It was still expensive, but she would make it work.

After they ordered, Roger said, "We can't stay in town long. We've got a lot going on back in California."

"That's right," Billie Jean said. "Your father has just gotten in on the deal of a lifetime."

Her parents talked about themselves, their financial success, and what a hardship it was to be in Vermont when everything was happening on the West Coast. Holly tried to look interested in what they were saying, but she didn't care about some software or some sort of special computers.

Billie Jean leaned toward her and held up her phone with a photo. "This is our house. Isn't it a beauty?"

Holly stared at the white two-story building that was more like a mansion than a house. She had to admit she was impressed. Her parents had done well for themselves.

"It's nice," Holly said. "Have you lived there long?"

"That's just one of our houses," Roger said. "We got ourselves a beach house in Galveston. And a place in Lake Tahoe." They continued to talk about their residences and how much they liked to travel.

Meanwhile, her thoughts kept returning to Colin. She missed him. She wished he'd have stopped when he drove by her shop. She was certain he'd seen her. He probably didn't stop because she was with her parents. She couldn't blame him. They were a lot.

And yet, she did her best to look interested as Roger and Billie Jean went on and on about their business, their home, and their life. Holly nodded where appropriate. She didn't have to say anything, because they just kept talking. She didn't know anyone could talk that much. Then again, it took the pressure off her because she didn't have to think of what to say.

She felt guilty for growing bored when they talked about their business. She told herself to act more interested. After all, this was what she'd wanted since she was a kid.

She cleared her throat, and when there was a slight pause in the conversation, she asked, "Have you always lived in California?"

"No," Billie Jean said.

"Yes," Roger said.

They'd spoken over each other. Then they both frowned at each other, as though they were confused about the disagreement.

Then Billie Jean turned to her. "Your father likes to forget that in the early years, we worked our way across the South until we settled in California. Once we made it there, we stayed."

"I hear it's nice," Holly said.

"It is," Billie Jean said. "You know what I heard at the B&B this morning?" She didn't wait for a response before she carried on. "There's a Christmas party tonight. It seems like it's the talk of the town."

Holly nodded. "The Kringles are having their annual Christmas party."

"Are you going?" Billie Jean looked eager for the answer.

"I...I don't know." She honestly didn't know. But without her grandmother there to prod her into going with her, she didn't see herself going alone. "Probably not."

"You should go." Billie Jean elbowed Roger.

"Uh, yes," Roger said. "It sounds like a good time."

"And don't worry," Billie Jean said. "You don't have to go alone. We'll be your guests."

"That sounds like a great idea," Roger said.

"Then it's settled." Billie Jean smiled like she was pleased she'd solved a problem that had never existed in the first place.

Holly sat there quietly while her parents worked out what time they would head to the party. All the while, Holly wondered how all of the sudden, she was taking her parents to a party where she would have to introduce them to who's who of

Kringle Falls. Her stomach took a nauseous lurch. This was moving faster than she was prepared for.

When the meal was finished, Billie Jean excused herself to visit the ladies' room. That left Holly alone with Roger. She felt less comfortable with him. And she didn't know quite why.

He pulled out his phone and started scrolling on it. She tried to think of something to say to ease the awkwardness, but the harder she tried to think of an interesting bit of trivia, the more her mind went blank. It appeared Roger had run out of things to talk about.

He glanced up from his phone. "I better see what's taking Billie Jean so long."

No sooner had he walked away than the server showed up with their check. They said they'd be right back for it. Holly's gaze kept moving in the direction her parents had gone. She didn't see them.

As the time passed and neither Roger nor Billie Jean returned, Holly glanced at the check. Her eyes widened at the amount. They certainly didn't live modestly.

As one minute turned into two and two into five, the server returned for the check. Holly inwardly groaned when she looked around for her parents, but they were nowhere in sight.

The server looked expectantly at her. Heat rushed to Holly's cheeks. She didn't have the money to pay this three-figure bill. But what choice did she have? With great reluctance, she reached into her wallet and pulled out her business credit card. She placed it in the check holder.

Had her parents left her? The thought sat heavy on her shoulders. After all, this wouldn't be the first time they'd abandoned her. She supposed she should be used to it.

Thankfully, the server was prompt, and Holly was finally able to leave. She headed for the exit. But before she reached the outer door, she found her parents. They were looking at the display of brochures of all the places of interest in Kringle Falls. Billie Jean had a few in her hand, and Roger was reaching on the top row for her.

A pent-up breath expelled from Holly's lungs. They hadn't left her. They just got distracted. And then she felt guilty for thinking that they'd abandoned her again.

When they turned around, Billie Jean smiled. "Sorry. I saw these and had to get some. There are a lot of new things in town."

Holly forced a smile to her lips but didn't say anything. She felt like a twisted pretzel on the inside. Being with these two made her feel like she was auditioning or something. The whole thing made her feel exhausted.

"I need to get back to the shop." She checked the time on her phone. *Ugh!* She'd been gone much longer than she'd intended.

"We'll see you this evening," Billie Jean said. "I can't wait."

"Uh-huh." Holly rushed out the door.

She walked as fast as she dared on the salted sidewalks. The cold air felt good on her overheated face. Since she'd ridden to the restaurant in her parents' car, she had to walk back to the soap company. She honestly didn't mind.

At last, she could take a full, deep breath. Her head ached. And she felt nauseous. All she wanted to do was go home, curl up on the couch with Tater Tot, and watch something relaxing on television. She didn't know two people could talk that much.

Instead of going into the shop like she normally would do, she went to the apartment. She rushed upstairs and ran to Tater Tot's crate. He greeted her with a wagging tail. When she opened the door, he ran into her arms and licked her face.

She scooped his little body up into her arms and moved to the couch. They sat there in the quiet, and she ran her hand over his back repeatedly.

"I don't know what's wrong with me," she said. "This is my childhood Christmas wish come true. I should be happy. I should be excited. And all I am is relieved to be here with you."

Tater Tot lifted his head and once more licked her face. Holly lowered her head and rested her cheek against the top of his head. She stared straight ahead and noticed the bare Christmas tree. It made her think of Colin.

Without giving it much thought, she reached for her phone. She dialed Colin's number. It rang once, twice, and then switched to voicemail. For a fleeting moment, she thought of leaving him a message, but on second thought, she ended the call without a word.

She sat there for a few more minutes with Tater on her lap. And then she said, "I think you and I need to get back to work."

"Arf-arf!"

She couldn't just sit there and let her parents' appearance in her life upset her. After all, they were making an attempt to establish a relationship with her. She had to make an attempt too.

CHAPTER FOURTEEN

I T HAD BEEN A day that wouldn't stop.

At least that was how it felt to Colin. After the emergency appointment that morning, he'd barely made it home, when he got called back to the clinic. This time for an intestinal blockage.

Charlie Baker brought in his black lab, Smudge. This wasn't the first time Smudge had eaten something he wasn't supposed to. First, they'd tried some non-invasive procedures to retrieve the sock, but it was too far in his digestive track.

After it was determined there was only one way to retrieve the sock, Colin called in only necessary staff. They were used to it. In fact, he had two teams, so they alternated who was on call on the weekends. He made sure they were well-compensated for the intrusion on their time off.

The surgery went without any complications. But he stuck around afterward to monitor Smudge. He was concerned because it was a big surgery for the playful dog. And even though he had told Charlie to go home and he would call him when the surgery was over, Charlie had remained in the waiting room. They talked for a while, and then Charlie grudgingly went home alone. Smudge would stay at the clinic and be monitored over the weekend.

It was late in the afternoon when Colin finally grabbed his phone from his desk and saw that there had been a missed call from Holly. She hadn't left him a message, and that left him wondering what she had wanted.

When he checked the time she'd called, he noticed it was after lunch—after her meal with her parents. He wondered how it had gone. For Holly's sake, he hoped everything went well. But he didn't trust Roger and Billie Jean. They'd had Holly's entire life to come back. Why now?

He went to dial Holly's number but hesitated. He slipped the phone into his pocket. Perhaps he should do this in person. He checked the time. If he hurried, he should be able to catch her at the store just before she closed up.

When he arrived, there were at least a half dozen people in the shop, filling their shopping baskets. When Holly spotted him, she smiled and held up a finger for him to wait for her. He nodded.

While she attended to the customers, he made his way around the shop. She had such a wide array of soaps. He liked that not only did she display their components but she also listed what the soaps were good for, such as dry skin or oily skin. She'd even added some alternative uses for the soap, such as a way to deodorize drawers or to repel animals from chewing on furniture.

In the end, he picked out a basket and a few bars from wood sage to sandalwood. He wouldn't mind giving them a try.

After the last customer checked out and headed for the door, he moved to the checkout counter. He placed the soaps on the counter before turning to add the now-empty basket to the stack of baskets at the end of the counter.

Holly's eyes widened as she looked down at his purchases. "You don't have to buy these."

"Well, I'm not just going to steal them."

She rolled her eyes. "What I mean is that you don't have to feel obligated to buy anything."

"I don't. I looked around, and I saw a lot I'd like to try. I thought I'd start with these."

Her questioning gaze met his. "You're sure."

He nodded. "I'll be back to try some others. I like that you have those signs above each, explaining different uses for the soap. I never would have thought of any of them."

She smiled as she rang up his purchases. "Glad you found them helpful. They were actually my idea. Gran wasn't so sure about it. She thought it might confuse some people. So, we didn't do it. But now that the shop is mine, I've made a few changes here and there. Gran always said when it was my place that I should go ahead and make it my own."

"I'm sure she would be proud of how you've changed things."

"I have other ideas, like remodeling, but that will take money, and I don't have it right now."

He looked around the shop and then back at her. "Someday, you'll have to tell me what you have in mind for the place."

She shook her head. "You don't want to hear about that. It's boring."

"Actually, I find remodeling fascinating. If I wasn't a vet, I think I would have been a contractor."

She arched a brow as she stared at him. "You know what? I can see that. You were always good with your hands. Okay. I have the sketches upstairs. Sometime I'll show them to you."

He nodded. "It's a date."

He didn't mean an actual date, but once the words were out there, he didn't want to take them back. He really didn't. But he also knew Holly was going through a lot right now, and he didn't want to make her life even more complicated.

She wrapped the soaps in tissue paper before placing them in a cute brown paper bag with the name: Kringle Soap Co. on the front. It had rope-style handles.

She held up the receipt. "Do you want the receipt? Or should I put it in the bag?"

"The bag is fine." He shifted his weight from one foot to the other. "How did lunch go with your parents?"

She smiled as she looked at him. "You know I saw you drive by at lunchtime."

"You did, huh?" Heat crept up his neck. "I was, uh, on my way home."

Her smile broadened. "I believe you live on the other side of town."

She'd made a very good point. Now what was he supposed to say? Perhaps the truth. Yes, that was always the best route.

"I actually drove over to see you. But then when I saw you with your parents, I didn't want to intrude."

"That was sweet of you, but you wouldn't have been intruding. In fact, I kind of wished that you would have been at lunch, but you would have been bored."

"Why is that?"

"Well, they chose The Peppermint Courtyard. I'd never been there. Gran never would have splurged on a meal. She always said there was nothing there that she couldn't cook at home." A smile flitted across her beautiful face as she thought of her grandmother. "And once we were there, well, all they did was talk about themselves. *A lot.*"

"So, I guess I don't need to ask how the lunch went."

She shook her head. "I feel guilty because I think they were trying. It's just that their lives and interests are so different from mine."

"It's okay. They live in a place far from Kringle Falls. Did you tell them some about your life?"

She once more shook her head. "They never asked, and I never got an opportunity."

"And how did you leave things?"

Her mouth gaped as her eyes widened. "I just remembered that they left me with the check."

He had to admit that he didn't see that coming. "They made you pay for your lunch?"

"No. I mean, yes, but I had to pay for everyone's lunch."

A frown pulled at his lips. "That couldn't have been cheap."

"It wasn't. I had to put it on the business credit card. My grandmother is rolling in her grave. She said that credit card was for business. Period. And she never would have approved of me paying for their lunch."

"Oh, Holly, I'm sorry lunch didn't go the way you'd hoped."

"Thanks. But they're trying. I guess that's something."

He nodded, but he didn't say anything. Holly was trying so hard to see her parents as the loving kind from her dreams that she couldn't see them as they truly were.

"Tonight's the Kringles' party," she said, drawing him from his thoughts. "Are you going?"

"Actually, that's why I came over earlier. I wanted to ask you if you'd go with me."

"To the party?" When he nodded again, she said, "Well, uh, my parents want to go as my guests."

"I see." The thought gave him an uneasy feeling. Even though he wasn't anxious to spend time with her parents, he felt that Holly just might need some backup that evening. "Then I guess we could go as a foursome. If you want…"

She was quiet for a moment, as though weighing her answer. Was she hesitating because she didn't want to hurt his feelings when she turned him down? Or was she concerned that her parents might not like her bringing a date?

"I would like that." She smiled. "Thank you. Can I just meet you there?"

"Absolutely." He smiled back at her. "I'll see you in a little bit."

And then he headed for the door. His steps felt a bit lighter. Had he just asked her out on an official date? He supposed he had. Too bad it was going to be chaperoned by both sets of parents as well as half of the town.

CHAPTER FIFTEEN

A DRESS FROM THE back of her closet.

High heels, also from the back of her closet. Holly felt nervous. Would anyone notice that she had on the same dress she'd worn to this party a couple of years ago? She hoped not.

She'd put on some makeup. It was more than she normally wore. Instead of just foundation, powder, and mascara, she'd also put on eyeshadow, eyeliner and a little blush. She'd finished it with some lip gloss.

When it came to her hair, she hadn't been sure what to do with it. In the end, she wore her long hair down over her shoulders.

And now, she stood off to the side of the party. The Kringles' house was filled wall-to-wall with festively dressed guests. Her parents had helped her carry the cookies she'd baked with Colin. Once the sweets were handed off to the people managing the food table, her parents disappeared into the crowd, leaving Holly on her own.

It was okay. It gave her a moment to gather herself. After all, this was her first time attending the Kringles' Christmas party without her grandmother. Her heart squeezed as she thought of Gran. Her grandmother loved this time of the year, and she especially loved this party.

Holly noticed Billie Jean never asked about her mother or her final days. Any time Holly tried to bring up Gran, Billie Jean would change the subject. Even if Billie Jean had problems with Gran, didn't she realize just how important Gran had been to her own daughter?

Holly wanted to say something to Billie Jean about her avoidance of the subject, but she didn't know how to bring it up without ending up in a heated argument. And that was the last thing Holly wanted. After all, her parents came to town for her. She had to do her best to make this work. Gran would have understood. Wouldn't she have?

"Hey, beautiful."

She'd know that deep, rich voice anywhere. She turned, and there Colin stood in dark jeans and a gray sweater with a white collared shirt beneath. His sleeves were pushed up, and the collar was unbuttoned. He looked good. *Really good.*

"Hey, handsome. Did you just get here?"

"Actually, I was here for a little bit. I saw you walk in, but I couldn't get away from Mayor Kringle. He has an idea for a parade next Christmas. You know how he is. He always wants to change things or add something new for the holiday." He glanced around. "Where are your parents?"

"Uh..." She glanced around, having lost track of them. And then she spotted them. "They are talking to the Gundersons."

The Gundersons owned the mill on the edge of town. When she glanced over, the Gundersons didn't seem to be saying much as Billie Jean and Roger seemed to be talking non-stop. She wondered if her parents were telling them about their life in California. Holly had been hoping the party would provide them another chance to hit it off, but her parents must have had other thoughts.

Now that Colin was there, she could feel herself start to unwind. He joined her as she got some punch and a small plate of cookies. Every now and then, she'd check her phone. She'd set up a camera at home to keep an eye on Tater Tot. She felt bad about leaving him home all alone. Thankfully, he seemed to be okay with it. He was asleep in his crate. Which meant when she got home, he would be ready to play when she was ready to crash on the couch and watch a Christmas movie. Luckily, he didn't have a lot of energy. An hour of playing, and then he'd be ready for bed.

In the meantime, she would enjoy spending time with the most handsome man at the party. They both knew everyone at the party. And yet, they mostly talked amongst themselves.

At one point, she spotted Belle with Parker. *Wait. What?*

Holly lightly elbowed Colin. "Did you know your brother was coming to the party?"

"Which brother? You know I have three of them."

"Parker. He's here with Belle. Do you think they're dating?"

Colin's head swiveled until he located his brother. "I have no idea. Maybe this has something to do with the dognapping."

"Shall we go say hello?"

"Definitely." He took her hand in his as they made their way through the crowd of guests.

But making your way through a crowd of partygoers is never a straight, uninterrupted line. And the party wasn't in one room. It was spread throughout the living room, dining room, kitchen, and four-seasons room. So, it took a bit to reach the spot where they saw Belle and Parker, but by then they were gone.

Holly lifted up on her tiptoes and looked around. She didn't see them. "Can you spot them?"

"No. I don't know where they went."

"Oh well. I'm sure they'll be back."

It was only then that Holly realized they were now standing next to Colin's parents. So, they talked with his parents, who Holly had always found so friendly. When his brother Michael and his date, Candi, joined them, they learned that there had been another emergency at Belle's house. They hoped that everything was all right.

Mrs. Gunderson stepped up to them with a smile on her face. "Your parents are delightful people. Tell them we're definitely interested in investing in their project. It sounds so exciting. But we have to leave now, Gerald ate the pizza rolls, even though he knows he shouldn't, and now he has raging heartburn." Mrs. Gunderson peered around the room. "Oh. There he is. Gotta go. Merry Christmas."

Holly looked at Colin. "A project? Do you know what she was talking about?"

He shook his head. "I don't."

Holly looked around. Her parents were talking to the Kringles now. *Please, don't let them ask them for money.*

Colin arched a brow. "Do you want me to scope it out?"

She worried her bottom lip as an internal war raged within her. "I should probably trust them, shouldn't I?"

Colin looked like he was stuck between a rock and a hard place. His gaze dropped to the floor as he shifted his weight from one foot to the other.

"Colin?" When he wouldn't say anything or meet her gaze, she wrung her hands together. Her empty stomach churned with nerves. "Colin, tell me what you're thinking. Please."

At last, his gaze met hers. "I just... Never mind."

"Come on," she prompted. "Talk to me."

"I just think that you've known the people in this room your entire life. You care about them, and they care about you. But what do you know about your parents? Maybe it wouldn't hurt to find out what this 'project' is."

When he put it that way, it sounded reasonable. And yet she hesitated. There was a part of her that didn't want to know what her parents were up to. What would she do if she didn't like the answer? Ask them to leave? The party? The town? The state?

"They moved on from the Kringles." Colin's voice drew her from her troubling thoughts. "Maybe I'll go have a word with the mayor."

While he was off talking to some of the guests, Holly made her way toward Merry Kringle. She couldn't ignore whatever it was that her parents were up to. But before she reached her, Merry was approached by someone else and they disappeared into the kitchen.

While Holly waited for her to return, she moved to the punch bowl. It was there that she bumped into Felicity.

Holly smiled. "It's good to see you again."

"I forgot what life is like in a small town—always bumping into everyone."

"Hey, Felicity, here." Justin handed over her phone. "You forgot it in my car."

Felicity's cheeks grew rosy as she took the phone from him. "Thanks."

After Justin moved toward the cookie table, Holly said, "You're here with Justin? Are you two back together?"

Felicity's eyes widened. "No. Definitely not."

"But your phone was in his car?" Holly arched a brow.

Felicity sighed. "It wasn't my idea. I'm working at the bookshop for the holidays, and well, it was snowing out, and Connie practically forced him to give me a lift to the school. It was no big deal."

"The school? You were taking a walk down memory lane?"

"Not even close. We were just at the school working on the Christmas play."

"Together?"

Felicity shook her head. "No. He's doing the set, and I'm working on the costumes, but to be honest, most of them are done."

"But you're spending time with Justin." Holly felt like they'd taken a step back in time. She was at the party with Colin. Felicity was there with Justin.

"I see my mother. I have to go. It was good to see you. Hope we can see each other again before I leave town."

Holly nodded. "I'd like that."

They hugged, and then Felicity walked away. No sooner was she gone than Colin returned. His face was drawn, as though something was weighing on his mind. She braced herself for whatever he was about to tell her.

When he stopped next to her, she said, "Whatever it is, just tell me."

"From what I can gather, Roger and Billie Jean are going around the room drumming up money for some sort of investment that has to do with some special computers."

"Are you serious?" The question was meant to be rhetorical, but Colin was nodding.

"I'm so sorry."

"Do you think this investment even exists?" She couldn't believe she had to question anything and everything about her parents, but until a couple of days ago, they didn't want to be a part of her life.

Colin rubbed the back of his neck. "I don't know. But it seems strange to me that they're trying to get money from ordinary people instead of a bank."

"You're right. They need to stop." Not taking time to think over her next steps, Holly headed for her parents, who were now speaking to Colin's parents. She stopped in front of Roger and Billie Jean. "You need to stop trying to get money from my friends."

"Sweetie," Billie Jean said, "you don't under-stand."

"I understand that you're asking my friends for their hard-earned money."

Roger looked a bit flustered. "You're blowing this out of proportion. We're trying to help your friends."

"I don't believe you." She reached into her purse and pulled out the bill from The Peppermint Courtyard. She held it out to Roger. "You owe me for lunch. You both skipped out before the bill came."

"We did not." Roger's face filled with color. "I was going to pay you." He glanced down at the bill. "But I, uh, forgot my wallet back in our room at the B&B."

When he made no motion to reach for his wallet, she knew he had no intention of paying her back. It was as though she were seeing them clearly for the first time. "This isn't right. You need to stop with the sales pitch. This is a holiday party. I don't know what you think you're doing, but it needs to stop now." She turned back to Tricia and John Bishop. "I'm so sorry."

Without hesitating. Holly turned and walked toward the exit. She needed to get out of there. Her chest was tight, and tears pricked the backs of her eyes. She refused to let anyone see her tears.

"Holly, wait," her mother called out. "It's not what you think."

She kept going, like she hadn't heard Billie Jean. She would have walked straight out the door if Colin hadn't appeared in front of her with her coat in his hands. She paused, and he held it out to her. And then hand in hand they walked outside.

The cold air felt good against her heated face, and at last she felt as though she could take a full breath. Colin drove them back to her place. Neither of them spoke on the short drive. Holly was too busy replaying the events of the evening. How could she have been so wrong about them?

Once in the apartment, she let Tater Tot out of his crate. He jumped up on her leg, and she bent down to pick him up. She laid her head against him, enjoying holding his warm, wiggly body. He was so sweet.

"Are you doing okay?" Colin's voice was gentle and full of warmth.

She nodded, even though she felt anything but okay. "I'm sorry to make you leave."

He walked up to her and gripped her shoulders as he stared into her eyes. "You didn't make me do anything. I chose to leave." His gaze searched hers. "How are you doing?"

She was about to be honest with him when his phone rang.

He held up a finger for her to wait. He checked his phone. "I have to get this. It's the clinic, and I have a patient there who just had abdominal surgery."

She nodded in understanding. While he stepped away to take the call, she put Tater Tot down on the floor and got him a treat. All the while, she couldn't help but think that sometimes what you wish for doesn't end up working out the way you imagined. This was one of those times.

Colin stepped into the kitchen. His brows were drawn. "I'm sorry. There's been a complication with Smudge. I have to go."

She wasn't ready to see him go, but she understood. "Sure. Thanks for everything."

He took a step toward her. Then he hesitated, as though not sure what to do next. He stepped back. "I'll, uh, call you later."

And then he was gone. She'd never felt more alone. After taking Tater Tot outside, she changed her clothes, turned off her phone, and curled up on the couch with the pup. She tried to chase away memories of her parents with a Christmas movie. It didn't work.

Chapter Sixteen

A DAY OFF...

Plus snow...

Equals a morning restocking the shelves and tidying up the store. With the blinds drawn, hiding the big lazy snowflakes twirling and falling to the ground, Holly turned on some Christmas music. "A Holly Jolly Christmas" played in the background while she worked.

At her feet, Tater Tot played with a couple of his toys. He had a little stuffed duck that squeaked. He would pick it up with his mouth and toss it into the air. Then he'd set off chasing it. He did this over and over again.

Holly didn't normally work on her one day off. But Christmas week started on Monday. She needed to be prepared for last-minute shoppers.

No matter how busy she kept herself, her thoughts were constantly returning to Colin. She thought she would have heard from him the prior evening after his emergency, but he hadn't called. She decided it was probably for the best because she wasn't up for talking. Still, she couldn't deny that she liked having him around. He wasn't complicated like Roger and Billie Jean.

What was she supposed to do about them? She tried to get closer to them, but they kept her guessing at their true intentions. It had her wishing they were still in California. And that just added to her guilt. Perhaps she was jumping to conclusions about them. Maybe she needed to slow down.

Knock-knock.

Holly straightened from where she'd been organizing a display shelf. Tater Tot barked and ran to the locked door. Who could that be? The Closed sign was in the window.

Her hand went to her hair. She hadn't done much with it that morning, other than to pull it back in a ponytail holder. And she was wearing some old sweats. Perfectly comfortable but not something she wanted people to see her in.

Knock-knock.

Tater Tot continued to bark. *Who is it? Please, don't let it be my parents.* She straightened her clothes and swallowed hard.

She crept toward the door. She peeked through a small gap in the blinds. She gasped. It was Colin. What was he doing there?

Her heart started to pound. She wasn't prepared to see him. But with the yappy pup beside her, there was no way he would believe she wasn't there.

With a resolved sigh, she flipped the deadbolt. She leaned down and picked up the puppy. When she eased opened the door and the pup spotted Colin, he let out some excited barks. The dog had good taste.

Once Colin stepped inside, she closed the door and then put down the wiggly pup. Tater Tot barked before jumping up on Colin. As Colin petted the dog, Tater Tot quieted. Her puppy was totally eating up the attention.

A minute or so later, Colin looked at her. "I hope you don't mind I stopped by."

She moved back to where she was rearranging a display. "No. Not at all. I've just been working this morning. What's up?"

His face creased with twin lines between his brows. He looked like he wanted to say something, but he remained silent. She wondered if it had something to do with her parents. She hoped they hadn't done something else to upset people.

The suspense was eating at her. "Colin, what is it? Just say it."

He shook his head. "It's nothing."

"It's obviously something." She straightened, giving him her full attention. "And I'm not up to playing twenty questions after last night."

He shifted his weight from one foot to the other. "I understand. I just thought you'd be upset about me having to duck out last night."

"Why?"

"Because it's that kind of thing that has ruined every relationship I've been in. The women say they love animals, but when the animals take priority over them, they are no longer on board with my job—with dealing with the interruptions."

She moved toward him and placed a hand on his forearm. "I'm sorry you went through that. But you forget that I've known you all of my life." She smiled at him. "I remember when you found a sick little kitten and brought it home. You wouldn't leave that kitten's side, even though the veterinarian told you the kitten wouldn't make it. You never gave up hope."

A little smile lifted the corners of his mouth. "And just to prove him wrong, Tiger lived to be sixteen. She was a great cat."

"You're a great veterinarian with a huge, generous heart. Don't ever make someone choose between your calling and them."

"I won't." He looked as though he wanted to say more, but he didn't.

"Do you mind if I continue to work while we talk?"

"Not at all. Can you use some help?"

She wasn't one to turn down a generous offer, since it was seldom one came her way. "Could you sort the soaps on the shelf?" She pointed to the one next to him. "Some people don't pay attention and randomly throw soaps in any old basket.

"Sure." He turned to the designated shelf and got to work. "Did you just make these?"

She shook her head as she organized a different shelf. "No. I've been preparing for Christmas for the past few months. I knew with it just being me running things that I had to be prepared. So, I spent the summer making extra soaps. And this fall, I created a bunch of gift baskets."

"Wow. I'm impressed. How is it that I didn't know you actually made the soaps?"

She shrugged. "It's an old family tradition. In fact, I still use recipes written out by my great-grand-mother, some by my grandmother, and then it skipped a generation." She didn't want to discuss her mother. "And now I'm working to come up with some soap recipes of my own."

"Are any of the soaps in the shop your own creation?"

She shook her head. "I haven't perfected any recipes yet."

"I bet you're just being a perfectionist. I'm sure they are good."

She shook her head. "They can't just be good. They have to be special."

"Says who?"

"My grandmother. My great-grandmother."

He smiled and nodded. "I understand."

They continued to work together for the next half hour. She couldn't believe he was taking time out of his busy day to help her with the shop. She appreciated it. No one she'd ever dated had lent her a hand like this.

After she finished sorting the last basket, she turned to him. "Thank you. I owe you."

"Good. I intend to collect now."

"Now?" She had no idea what he had in mind. She was hesitant when she asked, "What is it?"

He gripped her shoulders and stared into her eyes. "I'd like you to go to lunch with me."

Before she could answer him, there was a rapid knocking at the door. They both looked toward the door, but with the blinds drawn, they couldn't see who was on the other side. Tater Tot went into a barking frenzy as he raced toward the door on his little legs.

"Holly! Holly, are you in there?" It was Billie Jean's voice. "The lights are on. You have to be in there. Holly, open up." She resumed knocking, only louder this time.

The absolute last thing she wanted to do was open the door and let Billie Jean and Roger inside. She did not want to deal with them. She needed a day off from their special kind of stress.

"Do you want me to tell them to go away?" Colin asked.

She did. She really did. But she also realized that this was her problem, not his.

"It's okay. I'll deal with them." She walked to the door. Then she stopped and looked back at Colin. "Could you hold Tater Tot?"

Colin nodded as he strode over to her. Once Colin had the wound-up pup in his arms and was moving away from the door, she released the deadbolt and opened the door.

"Oh, Holly, there you are." Billie Jean looked relieved. "I've been out here knocking on the other door and now this one."

She wanted to turn the woman away, but she didn't. Holly pushed the door open wider. "Would you like to come in?"

Billie Jean didn't say a word as she hustled inside. Holly stuck her head out and looked around, but she found Billie Jean was alone. "Where's Roger?"

Her mother frowned at her use of her father's first name. "He had a headache. He's at the B&B, waiting for the painkillers to kick in. But I thought it would give us a chance to talk alone."

Holly got an uneasy feeling. She didn't know why. "I'm sorry, but that's not possible. Colin's here. We have plans."

Colin glanced up from holding Tater Tot. "Hello."

"Hi." Billie Jean smiled at him before turning back to Holly. "Can we talk? Please."

"Can we do it another time?"

"It's important."

Holly couldn't think of anything important they had to discuss. Her neck and shoulders tensed as she once more closed and locked the door. With reluctance, she turned to Billie Jean. "What do you need?"

"You." Billie Jean sent her a smile that was supposed to put her at ease but it didn't. "I want to apologize to you about last night. We should have told you about our project, and then it wouldn't have caught you off guard." Billie Jean sent her a pleading look. "We never meant to upset you." She reached into her coat pocket and pulled out some cash. She held it out to Holly. "Here's some money to cover the lunch. We never meant for you to pay. If it's not enough, let me know."

Holly took the money. She didn't stop to count it. Instead, she stuffed it into her pocket. "Thank you."

She was caught off-guard by Billie Jean's act of kindness. The stress she'd been feeling since last night eased away. Her neck didn't feel tense any longer.

In that moment, Holly felt guilty for jumping to the wrong conclusion about them. She wondered if it was too late to try to salvage some sort of relationship with them.

"I, well, we would like to invite you to lunch," Billie Jean said. "It's on us, and you can pick the restaurant. What do you say?"

"I, uh..." Her gaze shifted to Colin, but his back was to her as he worked to keep Tater Tot quiet. Her gaze swung back to Billie Jean. "I already have lunch plans with Colin."

"Oh. I see." Billie Jean sent her a knowing smile. "Colin, would you mind if we all had lunch together?"

Oh no. She didn't foresee this happening. Should she stop Billie Jean and tell her no? Or should she see if Colin was willing to go along with it? If so, then she could give them one more chance. This lunch surely couldn't go as bad as their last meal, right?

Colin turned. His gaze met hers first. She couldn't make out what he was thinking. Then he looked at Billie Jean. "Sure. We could make that work."

"Good." Billie Jean smiled. "Where would you two like to meet?"

Holly looked at Colin, and he shrugged. She instantly knew where they should go. "The Kringle Cup Café. It's the best in town."

Billie Jean nodded. "Okay. We'll see you there in say, an hour?"

"Sounds good," Holly said. After Billie Jean was gone, she turned to Colin. "I'm so sorry about this. If you don't want to go, just tell me, and I'll make an excuse."

He shook his head. "That's not necessary. I'll go." Then he gave her a quick once-over. "Are you going like that?" When she glanced down at her sweats, he said, "I mean you look adorable."

"Oh no. I have to go get ready." She ran to grab her coat. On her way out, she paused at the door and turned back. "Aren't you two coming?"

Colin picked up Tater Tot while she turned off the lights. She hoped this lunch went well. She knew they were running out of chances.

CHAPTER SEVENTEEN

Was it the right call?

Colin asked himself that question over and over as he waited for Holly to get ready. Luckily, Tater Tot was there to keep him company.

He honestly didn't want to go to lunch with Billie Jean and Roger. In fact, he could think of a lot of other things he'd rather do, like clean his bathroom or watch paint dry on his dining room wall.

And then he looked at Holly. He saw the flash of hope in her eyes when Billie Jean apologized for their other meal. He wanted this to work out for Holly, but he couldn't shake this bad feeling he had.

He couldn't help but think Billie Jean and Roger had shown Holly who they truly are. But either Holly was blind when it came to them or she believed in second and third chances, even at her own expense. He was worried about how she'd react when they once more showed their true colors. Whatever happened, he'd be there for Holly.

The bedroom door opened, and Holly stepped into the living room in a pair of jeans and a red knit sweater with a white silhouette of Christmas trees and reindeer. He couldn't help but smile.

"What?" She looked down at her outfit. "I wanted to look festive."

"And you do." He got to his feet and stepped over to her. "When I stopped by, I had two questions for you."

"What were they?"

"Well, the first is do you want to go to lunch?"

"And my answer is yes. I'm sorry we won't be alone. I just feel like if I don't get this right with Billie Jean and Roger that I'll never see them again."

He nodded. "I understand. And it's not a problem."

"Thank you for being so understanding. Did you hear her apologize?" A smile lifted the corners of her rosy lips. When he nodded, Holly said, "It meant a lot. So, what's your second question?"

"Would you like to go caroling with me—well, with some of my family—this evening?"

She smiled and nodded. "Yes. I would."

His gaze searched hers. "You don't have to say yes because I'm going to lunch with you."

"I'm not. I truly want to go. I haven't been caroling since I was a little girl. I used to go with my grandmother. But then as Gran's arthritis got worse, she couldn't walk all that way in the cold. She would tell me to go without her, but it just didn't feel right. So, I'd stay home with her, and we'd bake cookies and watch holiday movies."

"Gran was a special lady."

"I agree. We better go." After they were in his pickup on the way to the café, she said, "I have an idea. We can invite my parents to go caroling with us." When he didn't say anything, she asked, "What do you think?"

"That you should see how things go before you ask them."

She nodded. "Yes. That's good advice."

He found a parking spot close to the café. They arrived first, so they got a table in the corner. He resisted the urge to pull out his phone and start scrolling like he would normally do. Today, Holly needed him to be fully present.

He glanced over to find her rearranging the flatware on the paper placemat. "Relax. Everything is going to be okay."

"I know. It's just that nothing has gone well so far."

He reached out and put his hand over hers. He gave her a squeeze. "Stop worrying. If it doesn't work out, it isn't going to be your fault."

"But I keep jumping to the wrong conclusions about them. Maybe it's echoes of my grandmother, who didn't trust them."

This conversation wasn't helping her to relax. He needed to change the subject. "What are you going to get for lunch?"

"Uh...I don't know."

He reached for two of the laminated menus in the holder behind the napkin dispenser. He handed her one, and he took the other. For a couple of minutes, they quietly perused the menu. It wasn't like they didn't know it by heart after eating there throughout their entire lives.

"I'm going to get the club sandwich and fries." He returned his menu to the holder.

"That sounds good. Maybe I'll have it too." She handed him her menu.

The door opened, and in walked her parents. He had no idea how this meal was going to go, so he once more reached over to Holly. He took her hand in his own and laced his fingers with hers. Colin wanted her to know he was there for her. He would be her rock if she needed it. And if things worked out, he would cheer with her.

She glanced at him with widened eyes, but she didn't say a word. She didn't remove her hand from his clasp. In fact, she ended up squeezing his hand.

"Hello, you two." Billie Jean sat down across from Colin. "Sorry, we're late. We had an important business call just as we were going out the door."

"Billie Jean," Roger said, "we don't want to talk about that now."

She nodded. "You're right." She reached for the menus. "Did you two pick out what you're eating?"

"We did," Holly said.

Was it just him or did Holly's voice sound a little off? A little higher pitch than normal?

"Okay." Billie Jean scanned the front and back of the small menu. A couple minutes later, she said, "I know what I'm having."

Just then the server walked up to their table. Roger insisted they go ahead and order. By the time they got to him, he'd picked out a double-decker burger with onion rings.

And though the conversation was awkward at first, eventually the conversation turned to a trip down memory lane. Billie Jean told them what she remembered about Kringle Falls, since it was her childhood home. She'd run off with Roger at the age of seventeen. According to her, the place looked different—more built up—but at the heart of it, Kringle Falls was still a small town.

Colin only spoke when addressed. Other than that, he observed this strange and sometimes painfully awkward family dynamic. If he didn't know that Holly was their daughter, he wouldn't have guessed it. Holly smiled and laughed a couple of times. She was blatantly attempting to make inroads with them.

"Would you like to go caroling this evening?" Holly asked her parents.

His mother's mouth opened before she wordlessly closed it. She looked over at Roger, who cleared his throat. "I'm afraid we can't. We have important things to do."

Ouch. Did he just imply that spending time with his long-lost daughter wasn't important? Colin hoped that wasn't the way Holly took it, but one glance at her let him know that was exactly how she took it.

Holly pushed aside her half-eaten meal. "That's okay." She glanced over at Colin. "Are you ready to go?"

Even if he wasn't finished eating, he would have agreed.

"Wait," Billie Jean said. "We have some business to discuss."

Holly's brows scrunched together. "We don't have any business together."

Billie Jean narrowed her gaze on Holly. "We need to discuss the sale of the apartment and store."

For a second, Holly didn't say anything. It was as though the words had blindsided her. It took a moment for her to get over the sucker punch. But when it passed, her lips pressed into a firm line as she ever so slightly tilted her chin upward. Her eyes glinted with anger.

"There's nothing to discuss." Holly's voice was firm and clear.

"We appreciate you taking care of everything until we could make it back here." Billie Jean smiled, but it didn't reach her eyes. "But now we need the money for our next project."

"Taking care of everything?" Holly looked at Billie Jean like she was losing her marbles. "Do you even know what 'taking care of everything' entails?" Emotion made her voice waver.

"Well, you sold the house," Billie Jean said. "I hope you held out for a good price. We'll be needing all of the proceeds."

Colin swallowed hard. He wasn't one to get into people's faces. He liked to keep things civil, but there were some cases where that wasn't possible. This was one of those times.

"You have no idea what you're talking about." He glared at both Billie Jean and Roger.

Holly placed a hand on his thigh, stopping him from saying more. And he had a whole lot more he wanted to say to these two horrible, greedy people. How did these two heartless people get together and give birth to the sweetest, most thoughtful daughter? It boggled his mind.

This wasn't supposed to happen.

Her childhood Christmas wish of being reunited with her parents had morphed into a nightmare right before her eyes. Holly felt as though she'd been sucker punched. The food in her stomach sat there like a great big lump.

She felt gullible and too trusting. Why did she think they could start over? Why did she think these people were going to be genuine and caring?

She inwardly groaned in rage and frustration. She was so angry. Though that fury was mostly directed at herself. She shouldn't have let down her defenses. Her grandmother had warned her time and again not to trust her parents. Her grandmother had said it was a sad state of affairs when you couldn't trust your own flesh and blood, but it didn't make it any less true. Instead of remembering her grandmother's sage words, she'd let herself get all caught up in milk and cookie wishes.

Now that Billie Jean had ripped the rose-colored glasses from Holly's face, she could at last see them clearly. They were self-centered, greedy people. And she would never ever trust them again.

If they thought they were going to take her home and the business that her grandmother had entrusted to her, it wasn't going to happen. And not because she couldn't make a life for herself in another town, doing another job.

She would fight them tooth and nail because her grandmother would roll over in her grave if she knew these two worthless people stole the Kringle Soap Co., where her grandmother and great-grandmother had invested their hearts and souls. Holly owed her grandmother this much. So, if it meant spending every last penny, she would fight them to the bitter end.

"None of it belongs to you," Billie Jean said in an eerily calm voice, as though it were a foregone conclusion. "I was her daughter. *Her daughter. Therefore everything belongs to me. I know this won't be easy for you, but surely you didn't think you were going to continue to get a free ride, did you?"

Really? Holly reeled at the audacity of this lady. *How dare she think that she is deserving of anything that belonged to Gran?* Billie Jean didn't do one thing for her mother except cause her heartache.

Holly wanted to yell at their audacity. She wanted to have a total meltdown, but they didn't deserve that much energy. And so she summoned the persona she used when she had the most contrary customer.

"I don't think you understand," Holly said, restraining her anger. "There is a will and Gran left everything to me."

Roger leaned forward. "And I don't know how much money from the sale of the house you spent, but we'll be needing it. All of it. Don't try to cheat us."

"How dare you come here, demanding things that don't belong to either of you," Holly said. "You've been gone for years—for my whole life. You didn't love her. And you never loved me."

Anger flared in Billie Jean's eyes. "You don't know anything about love. It's nothing you can count on. My mother didn't love me after I broke her ridiculous rules. She didn't understand how much I hated this town and needed to find a place where I belonged."

A heavy silence fell over their table. Holly felt Colin's stiff body next to her. She hated that he'd had a front row seat for the final decimation of her family. After this moment, she was an orphan by choice, because these two people in front of her were not her parents. They didn't want to be her family. And she didn't want them to be her family. It was time to end this charade.

"I'm not giving you the apartment or the store." Holly's voice was low but full of angry vibes. "I'm going to give you exactly what you've given me throughout my life. Nothing."

"We will sue you," Roger said. "We will take everything you have."

"Do whatever you need to do." She got up and walked away.

She didn't know if Colin followed her. She couldn't pause to look back, because it was all she could do to hold her head high. Her legs had a mind of their own as she headed for the door. The next thing she knew the cold metal of the handle was in her hand, and she was yanking the door open.

It wasn't until she was outside in the cold air and snow that she realized she hadn't bothered to put her coat on. She couldn't go back. She couldn't face them again.

She kept walking. The cold air felt good against her heated skin. And at last, she could take a deep breath.

Her childhood Christmas wish was over. It was shattered into a million jagged ugly pieces.

Chapter Eighteen

H IS HEART ACHED FOR her.

Colin sat in the booth as Holly walked away with her shoulders straight and her head held high. She was the strongest woman he'd even known—he would ever know.

And everything within him wanted to protect her, but she hadn't needed him to come to her rescue. She was quite capable of taking care of herself. But that didn't mean he couldn't speak his mind.

He looked at the two miserable people sitting across from him. He couldn't tell if they looked disappointed because Holly hadn't just handed over the entire estate or angry because they knew she'd called their bluff.

"You two made the biggest mistake of your lives," Colin said. "You not only missed out on knowing your daughter, but you missed out on knowing the most amazing woman with the biggest heart. Instead of being proud of how she turned out, in spite of you missing out on her entire life, you come here and scheme and threaten. But if you think you're going to steal what her grandmother left to her, you're mistaken. You would have to fight not only Holly but this entire town. If you haven't noticed, everyone loves her."

He grabbed Holly's coat and stood. Their server was standing nearby. He approached her and reached into his wallet. He pulled out enough money to cover the bill for the entire table, because he doubted her parents would pay their portion of their bill, and he made sure to include a generous tip.

As he walked outside into the snowy afternoon, he realized something that he'd been denying for far too long. He loved Holly.

He knew it as certain as he knew the sun would come up in the morning. It was as though it were meant to be. She had been the girl-next-door—the girl who used to follow him around and help him with the strays. Now she'd grown into a beautiful, caring woman who lived across town—the woman who still cared about strays.

He looked up and down the street. He didn't see her. He headed for his pickup, but before he reached it, he heard someone calling his name. He paused and turned around. His brother Justin was headed toward him.

"Hey," Justin said. "Is everything all right? I saw the end of what happened in the café."

Colin paused and rubbed the back of his neck. "You saw that, huh?"

Justin nodded. "So did everyone in the café. But don't worry. You know that they're all on your side."

"I just don't understand how anyone can treat their own flesh and blood like that. They come to town and try to scam their daughter's friends out of their money. And then when Holly won't hand over her inheritance, they threaten to take her to court. Who does that?"

"I...I don't know." Justin stuffed his hands into his pockets. "Is there anything I can do? You know to help."

Colin shook his head. "No. I don't know what to do at this point."

"Are you sure? Because I'm in good with the sheriff, and we could run them out of town." Justin sent him a hesitant smile.

Colin sent him a half-hearted smile. "I'll keep it in mind, but right now, I need to go check on Holly. She stood up to them, but I could tell that it cost her—it cost her a lot."

Justin nodded. "Go. And if either of you need anything, let me know."

"I will. Thanks." Colin turned and continued toward his pickup.

A few minutes later, when he arrived at Holly's place, he was about to ring the bell, but then he decided to try the door knob. It turned in his hand, and he smiled. She'd left it unlocked for him.

He took the stairs two at a time. "Holly! Hey, Holly, are you here?"

When he reached the top of the stairs, he didn't hear anything. He started to worry. Was it possible that she wasn't home? But then why was the door unlocked?

Then he heard a tinkling sound. He followed it to the living room, where he found Holly. She was standing next to the Christmas tree with glass ball ornaments dangling from her fingertips. Her back was to him as she placed one of the ornaments on the end of a tree limb.

He didn't want to startle her, so he kept his voice low. "Holly?"

She turned to him. "Oh, hey, sorry I left you behind."

He stepped farther into the room. "It's okay. I understand. I brought your coat." He placed it over the arm of the chair before he stepped closer to her. "How are you doing?"

"I just want to get this tree decorated. I, uh...strung the lights the other night." When she reached out to put another ornament on the tree, he noticed the slight tremor in her hand. "If I could just get this tree finished, I could put away the boxes of decorations."

He moved to the coffee table. "Mind if I help?"

She still wouldn't look at him, but she nodded. "Go ahead."

After he took off his coat, he picked up a few ornaments. He moved to the tree and reached up high to place one. As he hung the ornaments on the tree, he glanced over at Holly, but she kept her face downcast.

In the background, he heard her phone ring. She rushed over to look at the screen, and then without answering it, she put it back down. He hoped it wasn't her parents calling to harass her.

He was worried about her. He couldn't imagine what she must be feeling. At least she had Tater Tot. It was at that moment that Colin realized he didn't see the pup.

"Where's Tater Tot?"

"Oh. I put him in the bedroom when I was getting out the ornaments. He kept jumping and trying to grab things with his mouth. I didn't want him to get hurt or for the ornaments to get broken."

"What if we move the ornaments on top of the stacked boxes where he can't reach them?"

She shrugged. "That's fine."

He went to the entryway and grabbed a couple of boxes. He noticed there were considerably less boxes than when he'd first come over. He smiled. She was starting to feel at home. And no one was going to take this home from her.

After he set everything up so it would keep the puppy out the ornaments, Holly let Tater Tot out of the bedroom. The pup ran over to Colin to say a quick hello, then he ran back to Holly. Colin noticed how the pup stuck close to Holly's side, as though he sensed something was wrong.

"Are you still up for caroling?" He hoped she said yes. She needed something to lift her spirits.

Holly shook her head. "I think I'll just stay home this evening. I'm waiting for my grandmother's attorney to call."

"Oh good. You got ahold of him."

She shook her head. "I called Mr. Price's office but voicemail picked up. The message said he was away from the office for the holidays. I'm hoping he checks his messages and gets back to me this evening."

He wondered if the man would check his messages. A lot of people would just let it go until the New Year. Colin made a mental note to ask around and see if anyone knew how to reach the attorney.

When they finished decorating the tree, he took a step back. "I don't know about you, but I think we did a mighty fine job."

She looked at the tree and nodded. "Not bad."

It wasn't a ringing endorsement, but at least she didn't hate it, because if she did, he'd have taken off all of the ornaments and started over again.

"Are you sure you don't want to go caroling?" he asked.

"I don't, but you should go. I don't want you to miss it because of me." When he hesitated, she said, "Seriously. Go ahead."

He shook his head. "I don't want to go without you."

"Thanks. But I am not up to it." She turned to look at the tree. "I have some administrative work I should do before the shop opens tomorrow."

He wondered if the work she had to do was that urgent or if she was just anxious to get him out the door. He didn't want to leave her alone, but he was out of excuses to stay.

He stepped up behind her. "Are you sure you don't want me to hang around?"

When she turned, they were mere inches apart. "I just need some time alone."

He nodded. "I understand."

And then he found himself reaching out to her and giving her a hug. At first, her body was stiff, but then she leaned into him. Her head came to rest on his chest. Could she hear the way she made his heart pound?

Her arms wrapped around his waist. He didn't know how long they stood there in each other's arms. As far as he was concerned, time could just stop. There was nowhere else he wanted to be.

It was on the tip of his tongue to tell her he loved her. He had loved her for a long time. He just hadn't been willing to admit it—even to himself.

The time had never been right for them—until now. He felt a fierce protectiveness toward her, even though he knew she was perfectly capable of taking care of herself. It didn't lessen his desire to be there for her.

What would she say if he told her he loved her? Would she smile? Would she kiss him? The words teetered at the tip of his tongue.

Or would she back away? Would she say that she didn't feel the same way? He choked down the words.

It wouldn't be fair to either of them to make such an important proclamation right now. She was already reeling from the fact that her biological parents were trying to steal the only home she had left. They wanted to rip away the business that her loving grandmother had left to her.

It wasn't right. None of it. And that was why he had to be patient. He had to wait until her feet were once more on solid ground before he tilted that very ground with his words of love.

Holly was the first one to pull away. With a resigned sigh, he lowered his arms. He knew he should leave, but he hesitated.

"Is there anything I can do before I go?" When she shook her head, he asked, "Do you want me to pick you up a pizza to have whenever you get hungry?" When she once more shook her head, he said, "I wish you'd let me do something."

"I'll be fine."

He wanted to say something to comfort her—to let her know that everything was going to be all right—but no words would come to him. With a resigned sigh, he turned to walk away.

He paused next to her. "Call me if you need anything. If you want to talk, I'm your guy. Any time. Day or night. Or if you need a food delivery, I'm your guy. Remember, I used to do that in college. I'm experienced." He sent her a smile. She didn't smile back. He took on a serious tone. "I just want you to know that I care. I'm here for you."

"I know." Her voice was so soft but not so soft that he missed the pain laced in her tone. "Thank you."

Without giving a thought to his action, he leaned toward her. Though he longed to kiss her rosy lips, he aimed for her cheek. The kiss was light and quick.

Then he turned and headed for the stairs. In no time, he headed out into the wintery day. Would she call him? He honestly didn't know.

With every step he took, there was something inside of him that said he shouldn't leave her. And yet that's what she'd asked of him.

There had to be some way to help her. And then he had a thought. He pulled his phone from his pocket and called his mother. She was well-connected in this town. If anyone knew how to reach Mr. Robert Price, Esq., it would be her, or she would know who had the number to reach him.

As he briefly explained the situation to his mother, he climbed into his pickup and started the engine. His mother didn't have Mr. Price's cell number. And so, he sat there as she asked his father if he knew. Together, they came up with two people in town who might have the phone number.

He got the phone number from the first person. And then he placed the call. Mr. Price was surprised when he took the call. Colin didn't waste any time. He explained the situation and didn't know what to think about Mr. Price's quietness. Was he angry that his holiday break had been interrupted? Would he do anything to help Holly?

In the end, Mr. Price told him he was on vacation, but he would look into it. He didn't say how soon or even if he would get back to him. There was a simple, *thank you for calling* and then the phone went dead. And Colin didn't know if he'd done anything to help Holly or not. He wouldn't say anything to get her hopes up.

Chapter Nineteen

N O CALL BACK.

No message. No nothing.

Holly was climbing the walls. She thought for sure that Mr. Price would have checked his voice-mail and realized the seriousness of the matter. But as Monday gave way to Tuesday and morning gave way to afternoon, she was starting to think that perhaps she needed to consult another attorney. But that would be hard because Mr. Price knew their family history. He'd been the one to draw up the will.

But if it took her reciting her painful family history, she would do it. There was no way she was going to roll over for Billie Jean and Roger. They would get the soap company and the apartment over her dead body.

The last two days had been very busy at the shop. It wasn't so much customers getting last-minute Christmas presents but rather friends who had heard what had happened at the Kringle Cup Café stopping by to make sure she was okay. It was very sweet, but she hated the situation was public information.

Colin had been one of the people who had checked in on her. She'd assured him she was fine. But she could feel herself shutting down and pushing him away. And it wasn't his fault. It was hers.

Tater Tot walked over to her and jumped up on her leg. She bent over and scooped him up into her arms. He pressed his head to her shoulder. She laid her cheek against the back of his head. He was just the sweetest.

Her thoughts turned back to Colin. She needed time, she told herself. Once Billie Jean and Roger left town—once she showed them there was nothing they could take from her—she would get herself together. She would be able to deal with her growing feelings for him. But right now, she couldn't admit those feelings to herself or him.

Buzz.

She pulled the phone from her back pocket. It was Colin again. Either he wasn't working at the clinic that day or he was calling her between patients. She'd talked to him two times so far, once at lunch and once after lunch. She felt the hint of a smile pulling at the corner of her lips.

Colin was such a great guy. He deserved someone who didn't have such a complicated life. It wasn't fair to pull him into her troubles.

And that was exactly what she was going to tell him when the shop door swung open and in walked Billie Jean and Roger. Tater Tot began growling. Holly tightened her hold on him.

"We have something for you." Billie Jean waved around some papers.

"Get out and take your papers with you." The phone, still in her hand, stopped ringing.

"We aren't going anywhere." Roger paused to turn the sign on the door to Closed. "We don't want to be disturbed."

"We've tried to be friendly," Billie Jean said. "We thought you would understand that you can't take what doesn't belong to you."

Holly stood her ground. "Leave right now, or I'm calling the sheriff."

"You aren't going to scare us off." With an angry glint in his eyes, Roger took a step forward.

His glare and his closeness were quite disconcerting. When her phone started to ring again, a quick glance let her know it was Colin. She pressed a button to answer the call.

"I want you to leave. Now." She hoped that her voice came across as firm and not shaky like she felt on the inside.

"We don't have to go anywhere." Billie Jean stepped up next to Roger. "This is our property."

"You're our kid," Roger said. "You're supposed to listen to us. So, make this easy for everyone and stop fighting us."

"I'm calling the sheriff if you don't leave."

"You go right ahead," Billie Jean said. "But I've got papers here that say we are suing you for this business." She looked around and curled up her nose. "Still looks the same. Oh, well, the new owner can fix it up."

"We need to look at the financial books," Roger said.

"No." Holly struggled to hold on to Tater Tot, who was now growling in earnest.

As they continued to imply that everything belonged to them, Holly moved behind the counter. She felt better having a barrier between her and them. Who were these people? Because she just couldn't imagine that she was related to them. Her mother was nothing like her grandmother, who had the patience and kindness of a saint.

Holly's arms were tired from holding onto Tater Tot, but she couldn't let him go. She was afraid he would get hurt if she did. It was so sad that she could imagine either one of them kicking a dog. The thought made her stomach turn.

The next thing she knew there were red flashing lights outside the shop. Normally, this would freak her out. Today it was a blessing. Thank goodness Colin had paid attention and realized she needed some help.

Neither Billie Jean nor Roger noticed the lights as their backs were to the window and door. Holly tuned them out as they continued to harass her.

And then the door opened, and Sheriff Bishop stepped inside. There was a distinct frown on his face. Billie Jean turned to see who had entered. Her eyes momentarily widened, but she didn't say anything.

"Go away," Roger growled, not taking his gaze off Holly. "Can't you read? The store's closed."

The sheriff ignored the man. His gaze moved to Holly. "I heard there is a problem."

Roger turned. He muttered something under his breath, but she couldn't make it out.

Holly nodded. "I need them to leave."

"You heard the lady. Time to go."

"We're not going anywhere." Roger grabbed the papers out of his wife's hand. "We have a right to be here. This place doesn't belong to Holly."

Sheriff Bishop stepped forward and took a look at the papers. "That is for a judge to decide. Right now, you have to leave and don't come back unless you're interested in visiting the inside of a jail cell."

Roger turned to Holly. "This isn't over."

"One more word to her," the sheriff said, "and I'm locking you up."

Roger focused on the sheriff, sputtering all of the reasons he had a right to be there. Sheriff Bishop handed the papers back to Roger. But Roger's arms were waving around as he shouted. The papers fell to the floor.

Sheriff Bishop didn't miss a beat as he directed them to the door. Just then Colin rushed inside. When his gaze strayed across Roger and Billie Jean, he paused and glowered at them.

"Keep going," the sheriff said to his brother.

Colin hesitated before walking over to Holly's side. "I'm sorry I couldn't get here sooner. Someone had my pickup blocked in, so I had to run across town."

That explained why he looked so winded. She hated that she'd needed help from the Bishop brothers. Usually, she could take care of herself, but having to hold onto Tater Tot to keep him from getting hurt by one of them, she was very limited in what she could do.

As she stood there, watching as the sheriff ushered those people out the door, she felt her heart being crushed. How was it possible they'd given her life? She didn't think she was anything like them. At least, she hoped she didn't resemble them.

Those were the two people in this world who she was supposed to be able to trust, to lean on. Her stomach roiled. She wished they'd never darkened her doorway.

All she wanted to do now was close the shop, take Tater Tot home, and curl up with him on the couch. In fact, she didn't see why that couldn't happen. Now that the sheriff and the others were outside, there was no reason she couldn't lock the door. After all, the Closed sign was already in the window.

She turned to Colin and held out Tater tot. "Can you hold him?"

When Colin held out his hands. She placed the pup in them. At least now Tater Tot had stopped growling. Instead, he was now washing Colin's face with his tongue.

She'd almost made it to the door when it opened. The breath hitched in her throat. *Please, don't let it be more trouble.*

When she saw that it was Merry Kringle, Holly released a pent-up breath. "I'm so glad it's you."

Merry's brows rose. "Is everything okay? I saw the sheriff pulling out when I walked up."

"Uh, yeah. It is now." She could already feel the tension in her shoulders easing. "What can I do for you?"

Merry smiled. "It's what I can do for you. I've found the perfect family to take Tater Tot. I just stopped by to pick him up."

"Oh." It was all she could manage because it felt as though she'd just been sucker-punched.

Colin walked up to them with a wiggly Tater Tot in his arms. As she looked at the sweet pup, tears stung the backs of her eyes. She blinked them away. She wasn't going to cry. Not now. Not in front of them.

Colin and Merry exchanged pleasantries. All the while, Holly was trying to deal with the shock that Tater Tot was leaving and never coming back. The crack in her heart kept growing, and she didn't know how to stop it.

She swallowed past the painful lump in her throat. And when she spoke, she hoped her voice didn't crack with emotion. "Merry came to pick up Tater Tot. She, uh…. She found him the perfect home."

"He's going to love it," Merry said. "They have a five-year-old son and a fenced-in backyard."

Colin sent Holly a puzzled look. Before he could say anything, Holly said, "Can I hold him?"

Colin handed Tater Tot over. She hugged the pup's warm body to her chest. He rested his head beneath her chin, as though he sensed this was their last moments together. The crack in her heart grew larger, and the pain radiated out of her chest.

Just keep it together for a little longer. She swallowed hard. And then she whispered, "You be a good boy." Her voice wavered. "I know you're going to love your new home."

She stopped there. She wanted to tell him she would miss him. She wanted to say she loved him. But she couldn't because she was about to lose her composure.

She had to keep it together. This was best for Tater Tot. After all, she didn't even know if she was going to have a roof over her head for much longer.

She handed Tater Tot over to Merry. The pup sent her a look, as though he didn't understand why this woman was holding him. She wished she could explain it to him, but she just couldn't formulate the words without breaking down in tears.

And then she thought of something. "I have a whole bunch of Tater's stuff upstairs. I can go get it for you."

Merry shook her head. "That's not necessary. You can drop it by the pet shop when you get a chance."

Holly nodded.

"Well, I won't keep you. I saw the Closed sign on the door. I was hoping I could catch you before you left." Merry moved to the door with the pup. "I appreciate you helping me out. Tater Tot looks like he had a good time with you."

Holly nodded, not trusting her voice.

"Well, thank you." And then Merry exited the building.

Tater Tot was gone. The dream of having loving parents was gone. Her grandmother was gone. Soon this business would be gone. And soon her home would be gone.

She locked the front door and then turned to walk back to the counter. The weight of the day landed on her shoulders, and she felt herself stumble. Colin reached out. His hands gripped her shoulders.

She righted herself. She only had herself to rely on. She had to get it together, but not today. Right now, she was grieving her losses.

"Holly, why did you let her take Tater Tot?" Disbelief rang out in his voice.

"It was the right thing to do." She kept her back to him. She didn't want him to see the tears pooling in her eyes. "He wasn't mine. And he's going to the perfect home."

"It might be perfect for another dog, but not for Tater Tot. He bonded with you. And even if you aren't willing to admit it, you bonded with him. You two need each other."

"I'll..." She paused and swallowed, hoping to keep her emotions at bay. "I'll be fine."

"What can I do for you?" His voice was full of concern.

"Thank you for your help, but you can go now." She was relieved she was able to get the words out.

"I don't want to go. I can do whatever you want...even if it's just to go upstairs and sit quietly on the couch with you."

It was so sweet of him, but she couldn't let herself get in any deeper with him. She couldn't forget Roger's threat to take this place away from her. Everything in her life felt as though it was up for grabs.

And she was busy putting up walls around her breaking heart. It was the only way she knew how to survive this juncture in her life.

She stopped in front of the checkout counter. She braced her hands on the edge of it. She lowered her head. "Please just go. And don't come back. There's nothing here for you."

"Holly..."

"No. Colin just leave."

There was a tense moment where neither of them said anything. And then she heard his retreating steps. The door unlocked and then it opened. When it closed, she turned around.

Her gaze spotted the papers Roger had been waving around. She went and picked them up. She didn't read them. Not now.

Instead, she glanced at the front door. Part of her wished that Colin had ignored her request and come back, but he hadn't. He was gone.

A tear splashed onto her cheek. She tried to tell herself it was for the best, but it didn't feel that way. Another tear fell onto her other cheek. In fact, she never felt more alone in her life.

CHAPTER TWENTY

THIS WASN'T RIGHT.

Colin hated leaving Holly alone. He wanted to pull her into his arms and hold her. He wanted to promise her that everything was going to be all right. But he couldn't do that. Because he didn't know how any of this was going to work out.

He walked with no destination in mind. He was too worked up to go home. How could those people go into Holly's shop and threaten her?

Anger and frustration balled up in his gut. He had to think this through because he didn't want to do anything to make things worse for Holly. But those legal papers had him thinking. He stopped in the middle of the sidewalk and reached for his phone. He pulled up the number for her grandmother's attorney.

Mr. Price didn't answer his cell phone. Colin didn't blame the man, since he was on vacation, but that didn't stop Colin from telling the attorney about the latest visit from Roger and Billie Jean. He also might have mentioned how distraught Holly was and if there was something he could do to stop those two that he would greatly appreciate it. He even offered to pick up the tab for the man's services.

"Colin, is everything okay?"

He ended the call and turned around. Justin stood there with a concerned look on his face. Colin let out a sigh. "What are you doing here?"

"I heard there was a commotion at the soap company, and I thought I'd stop by to make sure everything was all right. As I was driving down the street, I saw you standing here, talking on the phone. You looked pretty animated, so I decided to see if you were okay."

"I'm fine. It's Holly that I'm concerned about. You have no idea what happened with her today."

As they stood on the sidewalk, snowflakes swirled around them. At first, he resisted saying anything. But he knew that he had to calm down if he was going to think clearly and come up with some way to help Holly. And so, he told his brother about Holly's parents and how miserable they were making her.

"I can't even imagine having parents like hers," Justin said. "It makes ours look like the best parents in the world."

"Little brother, we do have the best parents in the world."

Justin grinned at him and nodded. "Yeah. I guess you're right."

"Thanks for listening. I need to get going." Colin back-tracked to the clinic where his pickup was parked.

He was almost home when he realized what he could do for Holly. He turned around and headed to Purr 'n Woof Supplies. But when he pulled up the lights were off.

With a resigned sigh, he turned around. But instead of heading home, he drove to the Kringles' house. It didn't take long to get anywhere in Kringle Falls. It was a benefit of living in a small town.

He parked in front of the Kringles' house. He rushed up to the front door and hoped he wasn't too late. After he pressed the doorbell, he paced back and forth.

When the door opened, Merry Kringle stood there with her brows scrunched together. "Colin, what are you doing here?"

"Can we talk?"

"Oh. Yes. Come on in." She stepped back, pulling the door wide open.

"Thanks." He stepped past her. "This won't take long."

After she closed the door against the cold breeze, she said, "You look like you have something serious on your mind."

He nodded. "I do. It's about Tater Tot. Have you given the puppy to the other family yet?"

"I haven't. Not yet."

He breathed a sigh of relief. "That's good."

"I don't understand."

"It's just that Holly and Tater Tot have bonded. She wants the puppy back."

Merry arched a brow. "She does?" When he nodded, she asked, "Why didn't Holly speak up?"

He understood Merry's hesitancy. "Holly had a lot dumped on her today because of her parents. When you arrived, Parker had just stopped Roger and Billie Jean from harassing her. He had to escort them out of the shop. By the time you showed up, she was feeling overwhelmed."

Merry hesitated. "I'll delay placing the puppy in the new home for a couple of days, but if Holly truly wants the pup, she's going to have to come for him. She's going to have to admit to herself and me that she truly wants him."

He released a pent-up breath. "Thank you. She'll be here. She just needs a little bit of time to recover from the damage from those people."

"I'm sorry to hear about what she's going through. I just don't understand how people can be that way, much less to their own flesh and blood."

Colin didn't know what to say to that, so he said nothing at all. But at least he had a chance of getting Holly and Tater Tot back together again. But he couldn't push Holly today. The wounds were too fresh. But tomorrow was another day.

Was it good news? Or bad news?

The following morning, Holly had been asking herself that question since she'd gotten the call from her grandmother's attorney. Mr. Price was very brief but asked that she meet him at his office in an hour.

It meant she wouldn't be able to open the shop that morning. But this meeting was of the utmost importance. It might tell her if she was going to keep her home and business. The thought of losing all she'd ever known was quite daunting. She never thought about moving away from Kringle Falls, but this just might be enough to make her pack up and relocate.

She pushed away all of the negative thoughts. This meeting would go well. She hoped. At last, she'd have some answers. Mr. Price would know if they had a case, right? After all, he was an attorney, and he was the one who drew up the will.

She'd changed clothes three times until she realized this wasn't court. It didn't matter what she wore. She turned around to say something silly to Tater Tot about her being so nervous, but he wasn't there. The spot on the right side of the bed was empty. Pain stabbed at her broken heart. She told herself he was happy with a little boy to play with and a family to spoil him, but it didn't ease the pain of loss.

She settled on a pair of black pants. The color seemed rather fitting. Not wanting to be too maudlin, she chose a white blouse. Then she couldn't decide if she should wear her hair up or down. Eventually, she settled on her usual ponytail. She didn't know why she was making such a big deal out of this meeting. After all, the only person at this meeting was going to be Mr. Price. And she already knew him. He'd helped her through the process of settling her grandmother's estate.

On her way out the door, she grabbed the papers her parents had threatened her with. She'd looked over them. They were filled with a lot of legalese, and it sounded bad—very bad.

She checked the time. When Mr. Price had called, she'd had all sorts of time to get ready. When she walked out the door, she had to hurry. Luckily, his office wasn't far from her place.

When she arrived, the desk where his receptionist was normally seated was vacant. The office was filled with dark woodwork and lots of brass. Landscape paintings hung on the wall.

There was a huge brick fireplace in the reception area. Above the large wood mantle was an equally large wreath. That was all there was for holiday decorations in the office. Still, everything was tastefully done.

Mr. Price must have heard Holly enter because he appeared at his office doorway. "Holly, come on back."

She shrugged off her coat and hung it out in the alcove by the door. Then she headed to his office. She fished the legal documents out of her purse and held them out to him.

His brow scrunched up as he looked at the folded papers. "What's this?"

"These are the papers they were throwing around in my shop. I didn't think they had a case until I looked at them. Now I don't know."

He took the papers. "Have a seat and let me look over them."

She sat down in a wooden chair and didn't know what to do with herself while he read the papers. She got out her phone to scroll through the cute animal videos, but she never got that far because she noticed that she had a bunch of text messages. There were more than forty of them. What in the world?

She never got that many messages. Surely they weren't all from Colin. She realized she hadn't handled things between them very well. She regretted sending him away, but it didn't change things. She just couldn't take a chance on starting a relationship with him and have it fall apart. Her scarred heart couldn't take anymore.

Still, that didn't stop her from opening the app. She found messages from Belle, Candi, Felicity, Sheriff Bishop... *Wait. What?* Why was the sheriff messaging her?

Sheriff Bishop: *Just checking to make sure they left you alone. Call me if you have any more problems.*

She was touched that Colin's brother would reach out to her. She replied to him.

Holly: *Thank you. Everything is fine now.*

When she flipped back to the summary of conversations, she noticed that Colin had messaged her. *A lot.*

She opened the conversation string but didn't have time to read them because she heard a noise from the front of the office. She turned to see if someone was joining them.

When she saw Billie Jean's face, she gasped.

"I'm sorry. They're early," Mr. Price said in a disgruntled voice.

Mr. Price got to his feet as Roger and Billie Jean joined them. Holly looked at him for an explanation as to what was happening. She didn't understand. How were they supposed to discuss a defense strategy with them in the office?

"Did you tell her that she has no case?" Roger asked.

"Please, sit down." He gestured to the two other chairs.

Roger and Billie Jean hesitated.

"Sit down," Mr. Price said in a more assertive tone.

They did as instructed. Roger took the chair next to Holly. Neither of them looked at her. It was like they were angry with her for not just giving into their demands.

Her phone vibrated. She didn't have time to look at it. She slipped it back into her purse.

"Thank you all for coming in today," Mr. Price said. "As the attorney who wrote up Anne Berry's will, I would like to clarify a few things. She was of sound mind when she wrote her final wishes. It was drawn up quite a few years ago, but I can assure you that she gave it due care. And she was in no way coerced. I would testify to those things in court."

Anger rolled off Roger as the attorney spoke. "It doesn't matter. We have papers that say Billie Jean is the correct heir to the estate."

"Ah, yes," Mr. Price held up the papers Holly had given him earlier. "I've had a chance to look those over."

"They're legit. Signed by a judge and everything," Billie Jean said.

"I see that. Did you know that judge retired last week? One day before he supposedly signed this document."

"What?" Roger jumped to his feet. He leaned over the big oak desk. His voice was more like a snarl. "They're real."

Mr. Price didn't flinch. He picked up the phone. "Shall we call the judge now?"

Roger backed down. "It doesn't matter. Billie Jean was the woman's daughter. She should get everything."

"Sit down," Mr. Price said in a firm tone, as though he were speaking to an unruly four-year-old. He put down the phone. "Sit down, now."

Roger hesitated but then did as he was told.

Mr. Price pulled out another set of papers from his desk drawer. He put on his reading glasses and adjusted them on his nose. Then he scanned the document until he came to the right place.

"This is a personal letter that Anne put with her will." He glanced at Holly. "You didn't know about it because there was never a need for it until now." He cleared his throat and began to read.

"Billie Jean, if you're reading this letter, it means you came back to see how much money you can get from my estate. You never had time for me in life, but now you think you are owed something. You are not. But just so you can't claim that I forgot you or overlooked you. Here is one hundred dollars." Mr. Price reached into an envelope. He placed a crisp one-hundred-dollar bill on the desktop and slid it toward Billie Jean.

Holly couldn't help but think about how much it must have hurt her grandmother to write this letter. Gran had a big heart. It was why she had all of Holly's friends call her Gran, even though they were of no relation.

Gran was loving, but she was also a realist. She didn't hang her hopes on rainbows and unicorns. She tried to relay that to Holly, but she still clung to her Christmas wish of reuniting her family. She realized now how foolish she'd been.

Mr. Price cleared his throat. "I attempted to send you this letter and the money, but after an exhaustive search, we were unable to locate a permanent address for you."

Holly waited for them to give the attorney the address to that big white house that she'd seen the picture of at their lunch at the Peppermint Courtyard. When neither of them spoke up, realization dawned on Holly. The picture they'd shown her wasn't their home. It was all made up, just like most of everything else they'd told her. They were nothing more than con artists.

Mr. Price leaned back in his chair. "You can waste your time and money contesting the will, but you should know that I will defend it vigorously just as my client would have wanted. And if you continue to harass Holly, I will bring you up on fraud charges."

Roger muttered something under his breath as he stood up. Then he turned to Billie Jean. "Let's go. We have places to be."

And that was it. They walked away without another word to either of them. As they exited the building, Holly could feel the weight on her shoulders lifting.

Still, she didn't want to get too excited. She looked at Mr. Price. "Is this it? Is it over?"

He nodded. "I did a little digging, and neither one of them has any money to take you to court. And even if they did. They would lose."

Mr. Price stood and stepped out from behind his desk. "You don't have to worry. Go enjoy your holiday."

Tears rushed to her eyes as she stood. She blinked repeatedly. "I can't thank you enough for all you've done. It means so much. How much do I owe you?"

Mr. Price waved away her offer. "Nothing. Consider it a Christmas gift."

It didn't feel right not to pay him anything after the way she'd interrupted his holiday. "Are you sure? I feel like I need to do something to repay you for all you've done."

He was quiet for a moment, and then he smiled. "I know. After the holidays, my wife and I will stop by your shop, and my wife can pick out one of your beautiful baskets of soaps. She's always going on about them. Would that work?"

It wasn't what she had in mind, and it didn't seem like nearly enough, but she nodded her head. "Yes, it will work."

And then because he wouldn't let her pay him, she threw her arms around the older man and hugged him. "Thank you for saving the only life I've ever known."

When she pulled back, he said, "Don't hesitate to contact me if they bother you again. I *will* bring them up on fraud charges."

By the time she left the attorney's office, she felt so much better. She reached for her phone to call Colin and tell him the good news. Then she realized she couldn't do that—not after the way she'd ended things between them. Her good mood deflated like a balloon with a slow leak.

Chapter Twenty-One

ONE TEXT MESSAGE.

One short two-word sentence. *I'm okay.* It's all Colin heard from Holly that day. Still, it was better than nothing, but he didn't believe her. And he didn't know if Roger and Billie Jean were still in town or not.

He had a hard time concentrating at work. At least it gave him something to do, instead of pacing a hole in the floor. He told himself that she was okay or she would have called him, but after her parting words, he wasn't so sure anymore.

After he saw his last patient, he couldn't take it any longer. He had to go see her with his own eyes. And he had the perfect excuse. So, he let the staff lock up as he slipped out the back door.

It was already dark out as he drove to Holly's place. The short days were one of the things that he didn't like about winter. But the Christmas lights in the shop windows and twinkle lights adorning the houses along the quiet street offset the dreariness of the early darkness.

He pulled up and noticed the soap company was still open. He checked the time. It wasn't quite five o'clock yet.

He didn't let the store still being open deter him. He was a man on a mission. A customer exited just as he approached the door. He waited until they passed, and then he stepped inside. He inhaled the layered scents from vanilla and cinnamon to sandalwood and jasmine. The many scents blended together and created a cozy ambience.

He looked around but didn't spot Holly. There were a couple of other people in the shop, looking around at the many different types of soap. He made his way back to the checkout counter.

Just then Holly stepped out from the back room, carrying a cardboard box. When she saw him standing there, her eyes widened. "Colin, what are you doing here?"

"I thought we should talk."

She shook her head. "Now isn't a good time. I have customers."

"This won't take long."

She placed the box on the counter. It was then that he saw the dark shadows under her eyes. It confirmed that he was doing was the right thing for her. He just hoped she agreed.

And then because he couldn't resist, he asked, "How are you doing?"

She shrugged. "Okay. I guess. The attorney came back to town and took care of things. Roger and Billie Jean don't have a case and left. Hopefully, they won't be back."

"That's good." He wanted to know how the attorney accomplished such a feat, but he'd promised to keep this conversation short. "I have it on good authority that Tater Tot is missing you something awful."

She didn't look at him. "I'm sure he just needs time to adjust to his new family."

Colin shook his head. "He's still with Merry."

This time her gaze met his. "He is? But why?"

Colin chose to ignore the why question and instead told her the best part. "If you want him back, Merry will give him to you permanently."

He wasn't sure what reaction he was expecting, but when she smiled, his heart thumped. Her smile was bright, like the clouds had parted, and the sun had come out again.

And then her smile faltered. "Are you sure? I mean, she said she had the perfect family for him."

"Yes, I'm sure. And the perfect family for him is you. He loves you. And I think you love him too."

She nodded. "I...I do."

"If you hurry, I think you can find Merry at the Gingerbread house contest."

She glanced past him. "It looks like my last customers just left. I can lock up now."

She did a few last-minute things before putting the Closed sign in the window. He hung around to keep her company. The truth was that he enjoyed being around her. He just wished she felt the same way.

As they moved to the door and she turned off the lights, she turned to him. "Are you coming with me?"

He wanted to, but he didn't feel it was his place. He'd come here to do what he'd intended, and now it was time for him to leave.

"I've got some stuff to do at home. Tell Tater Tot I said hi." And then he walked toward his pickup.

The visit didn't end the way he wished it would have, but at least he knew that Holly and Tater Tot would be reunited. He told himself that was the important part.

―――ele―――

She'd ruined things.

As Holly rushed over to the gingerbread house contest, she couldn't help but regret the way she'd handled things with Colin. He'd smiled, and he'd been kind, but she felt a distance between them that hadn't been there before. And it was all her fault.

When she arrived at the gingerbread house contest, she glanced around for Merry. She easily found her in the midst of a small crowd. Holly's stomach shivered with nerves. What if it was too late? What if Tater Tot already went to his new home?

Shoving aside her worries, she approached the group. It took a few minutes until she made her way to Merry. "Hi. Looks like you have a big turnout."

Merry smiled and nodded as she glanced around. "More than last year. It's great to see so many people coming out to take part." Merry's gaze settled on her. "How about you? Can I sign you up?"

"Uh, I don't think so." It was time to get to the point of her visit. "I actually wanted to talk to you about Tater Tot. I made the biggest mistake by giving him up. I heard you might still have him. Is there any way I can get him back?"

Merry smiled. "I'm so glad to hear it because he's missing you something awful. And my husband's allergies are a mess."

"Oh, no. I'm so sorry about your husband."

"He'll be fine. I gave him some allergy medicine. I'm just so glad that you and Tater Tot will be together."

"But what about the other family?"

Merry waved away her concern. "Don't worry about them. I'll find them another dog to adopt. I firmly believe dogs should go to the homes where they are meant to be. And Tater Tot is meant to be with you."

Holly breathed a sigh of relief. "You don't know how happy I am to hear that."

"I can't leave to get him until the contest is over." Merry's eyes widened as though as idea had just come to her. "I know, why don't you have a seat and participate?"

Holly shook her head. "I'm not very artistic."

"I don't believe you. I've seen those beautiful baskets you create at the soap company. You're definitely artistic."

Holly knew she wasn't going to win this argument. So, she went and looked for a seat. When she spotted Belle, she headed in that direction, until she noticed that her friend wasn't alone. Interesting. Very interesting.

She turned and went in the other direction. At last, she found a seat in the back of the room. She ended up not being alone because Melody James, who lived next-door to the soap company, sat on one side of her. And some other friends sat at the table. At first, she wasn't sure what to say about the mess with Roger and Billie Jean, but to her relief no one brought up the subject. Casual chit-chat about the holidays went around the table, and Holly remembered what she loved so much about this town—its warmth and compassion.

She worked on the gingerbread house and found herself enjoying it. She had Colin to thank for getting her there this evening. She missed him and wished he'd come with her. She regretted pushing him away. She wished she could take it back, but it was too late for that now.

Still, she had a lot to thank him for. She should get him a Christmas present. It was last minute, but surely she could find him a little something special. She'd go shopping the next day.

When time was up, she inspected her house. She'd selected a red, green, and white theme.

There were peppermint candy shingles. Red and green gumdrops outlined the roof. Small red and green candies with white frosting outlined the windows, door, and corners of the house.

In the yard, she'd made a tree of white frosting and sprinkled it with coarse green sugar. There were candy cane fences and gumdrop bushes in the yard. It wasn't perfect, but at least it was presentable.

When she won third place, she was shocked. She was presented with a white ribbon and a gift certificate to The Peppermint Courtyard, which she found rather ironic. She would give it to Colin because she couldn't imagine herself going there without him. And then Merry presented her with Tater Tot, who lathered her with kisses.

She didn't know until that moment how much she loved and missed him. From this day forward, they would be together. There was only one person missing from their family—Colin.

CHAPTER TWENTY-TWO

H E MISSED HER.

Colin heard from Merry that Holly and Tater Tot had been reunited. They were good for each other. And now he didn't have to worry about Holly being all alone.

At that moment, he was out finishing his Christmas shopping. He'd procrastinated picking out his Secret Santa gift for Justin. He couldn't decide whether he should get something silly or something more meaningful. And so he kept shopping.

With it being Christmas Eve, it appeared that he wasn't the only one to wait until the last minute to finish shopping. Luckily with the clinic closed for the holidays, he was able to head out first thing in the morning.

As he looked around, he still didn't know what gift to get his little brother. However, another idea came to him. He bought an ornament that resembled Tater Tot. He had it personalized *Tater Tot's 1st Christmas*. Happy with his purchase, he kept shopping.

He knew even with Tater Tot in her life that this was still going to be a rough Christmas for Holly. It was her first Christmas without her grandmother, and she'd been dealt the realization that a relationship with her parents wasn't tenable.

He wanted to do something to let her know she wasn't alone. That she might not have a traditional family, but she had people in her life who cared about her.

As he meandered through the various shops, an idea came to him. He bought the biggest Christmas card he could find. He would have all of her friends sign it and remind her of the people who cared about her.

He pulled up his family's group chat and began to type.

Colin: *I need your help. I want to do something special for Holly.*

Mom: *What do you need?*

Colin: *I bought a giant card. I'm going to take it to Kringle Cup Café for people to sign.*

Mom: *See you there.*

All of his brothers and even his father chimed in that they would stop by and sign it. He thanked them. Since meeting Holly's parents, he appreciated his family even more than he did before.

And in that moment, he knew what he wanted to get Justin for Christmas. He headed to Jingle Bell Books. His brother always had his nose in a book.

But when he got there, he realized he didn't know what books his brother had already read. So, he would get him a gift card.

When he moved to the checkout counter, he was surprised to find Felicity working there. She had been Justin's girlfriend in high school. She was lovely, and they'd made a cute couple. And then something had happened and they'd broken up. Justin had been scant on the details.

Colin picked out a gift card and placed it on the counter. "Hey, it's good to see you."

She smiled back at him. "It's good to be back."

She rang up the gift card, and then a thought came to him: Felicity used to be one of Holly's good friends. Back in those days, the Bishop house was always full of kids hanging out. And his parents loved it.

After he'd paid for the gift card, he asked, "Would you like to sign a Christmas card for Holly Berry? I know she's one of your friends and well, this is her first Christmas without her grandmother, and I want her to know that there's a whole town that has her back."

"Oh sure. I'd be happy to sign it."

He pulled it out and placed it on the counter. "And if you could let your friends know, I'm heading to Kringle Cup Café with it for an hour or two."

"I'd be happy to do that." She reached for a pen. "What a thoughtful idea."

After she signed the card, Connie Carmichael, the owner of Jingle Books, signed it as well. And then he headed for the Kringle Cup Café. It was the most popular spot in town.

He didn't have to do anything but talk to the people as they lined up to sign the card. Once people signed it, they would message other people to stop by and sign it. In the end, the whole inside and back of the card were filled with heartwarming notes for Holly.

He hoped the card would show her that just because Roger and Billie Jean were her blood, it didn't make them her family. But the people signing the card, they would be there for her. They would be her family by choice.

And he would be there for her—if she'd let him.

With the card signed, he stopped at his house to wrap the ornament. Then he headed to Holly's apartment. He hoped she liked what he'd gotten her.

He had one more thing for her—his love. He was going to tell her he loved her. His stomach knotted up. He didn't know how she'd react. He would take his chances. She was worth it.

But when he got to her apartment, she wasn't home.

It had to be special.

Holly wanted a Christmas gift to show Colin that she was sorry for shoving him away. She wanted him to know that he was special to her—very special.

After closing the shop early, she'd tramped through the stores for a couple of hours. At one point, she'd spotted Colin but he hadn't seen her. She'd ducked out of sight. She wasn't ready to see him, not yet.

She'd browsed through the men's store, but a sweater didn't say special to her, nor did a hat or a shirt. She'd even made her way through the candy shop. Of course, there were a lot of temptations from peanut butter cups to watermelon drops. And yet as delicious as the choices were, they still weren't what she was searching for.

After leaving the candy shop, she walked along the sidewalk with no particular destination in mind. The snow began to fall, putting a light layer on the ground. It was beginning to look a lot like Christmas.

When she looked up, she saw Mr. Price heading toward her. A smile immediately pulled at her lips.

As they neared each other, she said, "Merry Christmas. Thank you again for coming back to town and helping me deal with Roger and Billie Jean."

"I take it they haven't bothered you?"

"No, they haven't. I'm so glad you got my message."

His bushy brows rose. "Your message? I didn't get a message from you."

"Then how did you know I needed your help?"

"He didn't tell you?" When she shook her head, Mr. Price said, "Colin called me and explained the situation."

"Wait. Colin called you? About me?"

He nodded. "Yes, he did. You have a great guy there."

She smiled and nodded. But he wasn't hers. The thought panged her heart. "He is the best."

After they wished each other a good holiday, she continued walking until she reached the card shop. She meandered around, looking at the ornaments, the Christmas decorations, and the cards. She made her way to the back of the store.

It was there she found colorful gift bags, ribbons, and bows. And then she stumbled across a selection of journals. She paused and looked at them in shades of pink and blue, and then she spotted a black and white one with a paw print on it.

She picked it up and opened it. Inside were blank lined pages, and she could envision Colin writing stories of the animals that he'd helped. The thought made her smile.

She also picked out a pen set for him to write his stories. On the way to the checkout, she noticed a mug with a dog and cat on it. It too made her smile.

After she put everything on the counter, she realized she didn't have anything to wrap it with. She asked the clerk to hang on a moment. Holly ran to the back of the store and grabbed a gift bag, tissue paper, and bows.

After she paid for her purchases, she made her way to the grocery store, where she picked up some dog and cat treats, as well as some apples and carrots.

With a smile on her face, Holly headed home. Were they expensive gifts? No. Would that matter to Colin? She didn't think so. Colin was never one who cared about appearances. He cared more about how people treated each other and their pets.

She did hope that in some way, they would show Colin how much she cared about him. She placed the gifts for the animals in a woven basket. She loved how the carrot greens lay over the edge of the basket and fell down over the side. The snack bags, she stood up in the back of the basket. And then the apples. She arranged them on the other side of the basket from the carrots. She affixed a large red bow on the handle, and it was done.

She wrapped Colin's gifts in tissue paper before placing them in the gift bag. She also added the gift card she'd won to the Peppermint Courtyard. But there was something missing. It took her a moment, then she realized that she'd been in a card store and walked out without a card. Who does that?

She had some blank cards in the shop downstairs to go with the gift baskets. They weren't what she wanted, but it was the message that mattered, right?

She told Tater Tot to stay. He didn't like being left out of anything, but he sat back down. She ran to the shop. Minutes later, she returned with a small white card with a simple wreath on the front. Now it was up to her to make the card convey her feelings.

With a pen in hand, she stared at the blank white space. She had to decide between keeping things light or telling him what was truly in her heart.

The answer came instantly. After all he'd done for her, he deserved the full truth. And so, she began writing, and then she realized she was running out of room to write everything that was in her heart. Who knew she was so long-winded?

She finished with: *Love, Holly.*

Then she turned to Tater Tot. "Well, little boy, it's time to go out in the cold."

The pup gave her one of his side-eyed looks. He was not wild about the cold.

"It won't be that bad." She put on his red and green plaid coat as well as his little boots. When he whined, she said, "But we have to deliver these Christmas presents. They're very special."

She just hoped Colin would feel the same way. With Tater by her side, she drove to Colin's house.

She turned on Christmas carols and sang. Tater Tot wasn't a fan of her singing so he laid down and pretended to be asleep, but she knew he was anxious to visit with Colin's dogs.

The drive was short. Once she parked, it took a bit for her to get herself, Tater Tot, and the gifts out of the car. At last, they made it up the slick steps to the front door.

With her heart racing, she knocked. There was a chorus of barks, but there weren't any sounds of footsteps. When there was no answer, she knocked again. And there were more barks.

He wasn't home. Disappointment slammed into her.

CHAPTER TWENTY-THREE

H E WAS DEFLATED.

Colin thought about leaving the Christmas card and ornament on Holly's doorstep, but he was afraid the wind and weather would get to them first. Plus, there was a selfish part of him that wanted to witness her opening them.

He wanted to see her eyes light up. He wanted to see her amazing, wondrous smile. Nobody had a smile like hers. It warmed him from the inside out.

He would wait to give her the gifts because when he finally saw her, he wanted to walk up to her and pull her into his arms and...

His thoughts screeched to a stop as he pulled up in front of his house and saw Holly standing there. This was his chance. His chance to play out his fantasy, instead of just thinking about it.

He barely pulled off the road. There was no time for perfect parallel parking. He wasn't even sure he'd turned off the engine as he hopped out of the pickup. His heart was pounding so hard it echoed in his ears, drowning out any other sounds.

He rushed up the steps, taking them two at a time. How could he not? Holly was standing at the top of them with that smile of hers that caused his heart to beat out of rhythm.

"Colin, I…"

He didn't stop to think that this could be the biggest mistake of his life. He didn't let himself think that he might end up losing any sort of relationship with Holly.

Instead, he wore his heart on his sleeve. Her mouth gaped when he took her into his arms. "Holly Berry, I love you."

He dipped his head and claimed her lips with his own. At first, she didn't move. He worried that perhaps he'd taken things too fast and scared her away. But then her lips moved beneath his.

He tightened his hold on her, drawing her closer. Her hands wrapped around the back of his neck as she kissed him back. His heart thump-thumped hard against his ribs. This moment with her lips on his was so much better than anything his mind could have dreamed up.

"Arf! Arf!"

Tater Tot picked that moment to grow bored. He jumped up between them. The moment was ruined, but it left the promise that there were more kisses to come.

Colin looked down at the pup. "You have terrible timing."

Holly let out a laugh. It was a melodious sound. It was a sound he wanted to hear the rest of his life.

When he saw Holly was shivering, it prompted him to unlock the front door and get them inside. His three dogs barked their greeting. Tater Tot joined in the dog chorus.

"Enough!" When they didn't listen, he said, "Quiet!"

His three went silent, leaving Tater Tot barking a solo. Holly shushed him. Tater wanted down, and he wouldn't quiet until his feet touched the floor.

Colin turned his attention back to Holly. He was waiting for her to say something about his proclamation. And yet, she remained quiet. Did this mean that she didn't feel the same way?

The thought made his heart still in his chest. But then he thought about her kissing him. She wouldn't have done that unless she felt something for him. Maybe it was because he'd done the one thing he'd been trying to avoid—he'd rushed her.

So, where did things go from here? He wanted to ask her, but he didn't dare. He'd pushed her enough for one day. The fact that she was still in his house had to be a good sign.

After they took off their coats and boots, he led her to a couch in the living room. He sat down next to her. "What brought you here?" When she jumped up and headed toward the door, he followed her. "Where are you going?"

She didn't say anything as she opened the front door. In stocking feet, she stepped out onto the porch. A second later, she returned with a basket and a gift bag.

She smiled at him. "These are for you."

"Hold that thought for a moment." He slipped on his boots and rushed outside.

It was snowing out. Maybe he should have paused to put on his coat. Then again, *nah*. He just had to grab her gifts from his pickup. His stomach knotted. What if she didn't like them? Maybe he should have gone with something more romantic like roses and chocolates. *Wait. No.* That was Valentines.

With the card in one hand and the ornament in the other, he bounded up the porch steps and inside the house. He pushed the door closed.

Holly stepped up to him and lifted up on her tiptoes. She brushed the snow from his hair and then his shoulders. Then she stared into his eyes, causing his heart to slam into his chest. For a moment, he thought she was going to kiss him. Instead, she pulled back.

He slipped off his boots. "Let's go in the living room. I'll start the fireplace."

He'd had a gas fireplace installed, so all it took was the flip of a switch to ignite the gas. Flames danced over the ceramic logs. It wouldn't take long until the room warmed up.

He joined Holly on one of the couches. "Now what were you saying?"

She held out a basket heaped with goodies. "Here you go."

He smiled as he took it from her. "How did you know I was craving carrots?" He picked up one of the snack packs. "And salmon slivers?"

"They aren't for you, silly." She smiled and shook her head.

"They aren't?" He feigned a pout.

"No. They are for the furbabies."

"Well, thank you. They're going to love all of those goodies." He got up. He placed the basket up on a shelf, out of reach of the dogs, and then returned to his spot on the couch.

"Go ahead," he said. "Open one of your gifts."

Holly hesitated. "Maybe we should save them for Christmas morning."

Colin shook his head. "We have other things to do on Christmas."

"We do?" She sent him a confused look. "Such as?"

"You're invited to my parents' for Christmas day."

"What? But I can't. I don't want to intrude."

"You won't intrude. They invited you."

"But I... I don't have a gift for them."

Colin moved to the Christmas tree and knelt down. He picked up the basket Holly had put together for him to give to his mother. With it in his arms, he straightened. "You can give her this."

She was quiet for a moment, most likely figuring out another excuse for not going. She could try, but he was going to keep countering every one of her worries. This Christmas, she wasn't going to be alone.

"But what will you give your mother?"

"I picked up a little something while I was shopping today. Now, it's settled. You're going to spend

Christmas with the Bishops." He looked at the presents he'd gotten her. "Open the little one."

She unwrapped it as though she were going to reuse the wrapping paper. He sat back and let her do it her way. He was in absolutely no rush. He wanted this evening to go on forever. It didn't get any better than this with the two of them together, surrounded by the furbabies, as the falling snow coated Kringle Falls in a fresh layer of fluffiness.

Holly held up the ornament. It dangled from her finger. "It kind of looks like Tater Tot. And you had it personalized. Aww... thank you. I will always cherish it because it'll remind me of this very special Christmas."

"Now, open the big one."

She looked at the giant envelope leaning against the back of the couch. "Is that really a card?"

"Open it and find out."

She opened the envelope and then pulled out the two feet by three feet card with a snowman on the front. The sight of it made her smile. "He's adorable. But why is it so big?"

"You'll see. Open it."

And so she did. She gasped. There were notes and signatures over every inch of paper.

Her wide-eyed stare moved to him. "I can't believe you did this. What did you do? Stand in the middle of the street and accost everyone to sign it?"

"Of course not. People heard about what happened with Roger and Billie Jean. They wanted you to know that you always have family and people who have your back."

Holly kept reading the notes on the card. When she glanced at him, there were tears in her eyes. "Thank you. I'll never feel alone again."

"No, you won't." He moved closer and leaned toward her. "Because you will always have me." Then he gave her a brief kiss.

When she leaned back, she said, "It's your turn to open your presents."

He picked up the decorative bag. He started to open the card, but Holly redirected him to the gifts. He loved the journal and pens. He'd never thought about writing down some of his experiences with the animals and sometimes their owners. He had some interesting stories to jot down. He'd definitely work on it.

And then it was time for the card. He wondered why she'd made him wait until the end to open it. He pulled out the card with the simple wreath on the front. He opened it and started to read:

Colin,

You were the boy-next-door who stole my heart with your warm laugh, your generous spirit, and the way you made me feel seen. I don't know if you knew it, but I had the biggest crush on you.

I thought I'd gotten over it, and then you helped me with Tater Tot. You haven't changed since you were a kid. You still have the biggest heart. And I've found myself falling for you all over again.

It was a long way to say that I love you. I loved you as a kid, and now I love you as a woman. And I hope you have a very special Christmas.

Love, Holly

His gaze rose to meet hers. "You do?"

She smiled and nodded. "I love you."

He breathed his first full breath since his big confession to her. "That's good. I was starting to worry that I'd made a mistake with my big show of sweeping you off your feet."

Her smile broadened. "Not at all. It was very romantic."

"Good. I have one more present for you."

"Another?"

He got to his feet and held his hand out to her. She placed her hand in his, and he helped her to her feet. He led her over to the Christmas tree. He took a sprig of mistletoe from the tree and held it over their heads.

"You're standing under the mistletoe." He grinned at her.

"I guess this means I better kiss you."

"Yes, it does. I might be taking out stock in the company that sells mistletoe. I'm going to need some year-round."

"Oh hush and kiss me."

"Yes, ma'am." He ducked his head and pressed his lips to hers.

Epilogue

It had been a day of firsts.

Holly had spent her first holiday with the Bishops. They were a big, loud, loving family. And they never let her feel like she was an outsider.

It was her first Christmas without her grandmother. Holly liked to think her grandmother would have been happy about how it had worked out. Gran always did have a soft spot for Colin. She would give him the last cookie because she knew how much he enjoyed them—she would make him lunch after he mowed her yard because, as she said, "He's a growing boy." A smile tugged at the corners of Holly's lips as she thought of her grandmother.

Holly had her first Christmas photo taken with Colin. It appeared to be one of the Bishop's traditions. Everyone wore a Santa hat and had their picture taken in front of the Christmas tree. Tricia, Colin's mother, pulled out the photo albums to show her pictures of Colin as a kid wearing a Santa hat. He was so cute, even back then.

It was also her first Christmas with Tater Tot. Colin's parents had graciously invited him too. After such an exciting day, Tater Tot was now curled up between Michael's puppy, Tank and Belle's puppy, Odie. The three puppies were reunited for Christmas.

With three puppies asleep in front of the fireplace, they looked Christmas card perfect. Holly made sure to take their picture. It was worthy of being framed.

And Holly played her first game of charades that afternoon. She was teamed up with Colin, and to put it mildly, they didn't win. But they did laugh. A lot. It felt really good. So much better than staying home and thinking of how much she missed her grandmother.

"Are you ready for dinner?" Tricia asked her.

Dinner? Hadn't they just cleaned up after the huge lunch? Holly's stomach was still full, but she wasn't about to admit it.

Instead, she plastered a smile on her face. "Of course. How can I help you?"

Tricia waved off her offer. "No help is necessary. I'll have it on the table in no time."

"Okay. Thank you so much for everything. It was a wonderful Christmas."

Tricia stepped up to her and hugged her. "We're so happy you spent the day with us. I've never seen Colin happier."

Holly hugged her back. "Thank you for having me."

She loved being there. She loved Colin. And she loved his family. Even if his youngest brother had been completely distracted. Something was going on with Justin, but whatever it was, he wasn't talking about it.

As Tricia walked away, the heat from the fireplace started to get to Holly. She quietly slipped on her coat and stepped out onto the porch.

She inhaled the cold air and immediately smelled snow. Even though there was close to a foot of snow on the ground, it smelled like there would be a fresh coating by morning.

She stood there, leaning against a post and staring out at the pristine snow. Her heart was full, and there was nothing she needed. She was grateful for this Christmas and for all the love that had filled in the cracks in her heart, making it whole once more.

"And what are you doing out here." Colin's voice came from behind her.

She turned to him. "I just needed a breather after that last round of charades."

"We're going to practice before next year." He smiled at her. "We can do better."

She laughed. "I don't know if any amount of practice is going to help us."

He sighed. "We were pretty bad, huh?"

She laughed again. "We were awful."

"I don't know if I'd go that far." He stepped closer to her and wrapped his arms around her waist. "Do you know what I'm thinking now?"

She loved this playful side of him. After all of the stress and disappointment of dealing with her parents, it felt good to let go and enjoy the holiday.

"You're planning to go sled riding."

"What?" His brows rose high on his forehead. "Maybe it's you who is bad at charades."

"Hey." She lightly slapped his bicep. "I am not. But charades isn't about trying to read each other's minds."

"It isn't? So, that's why I kept getting it all wrong."

She smiled and shook her head. "What I think you should do now is kiss me."

"Kiss you?" His voice was soft and charming. "Well, I don't know."

"Colin…"

He was teasing her and enjoying every moment of it. "So, would you rather have a kiss or a present?"

Her eyes widened. "A present?"

He pulled a small box out of his pocket and handed it to her. "You got me another gift? But I don't have anything else for you."

"Just open it."

She felt guilty. She should have known that he'd do something like this. But at his prodding, she unwrapped the small package and found a small black velvet box.

Her stomach quivered with nerves. It was too big for a ring box. Still, he'd gotten her jewelry.

She pried the box open. And stared inside at… Wait. Is that a blue dog collar with white crystals?

She picked it up, and a little silver dog bone dangled from the collar.

She sent Colin a puzzled look. "You got me a dog collar?"

He let out a laugh. "It's for Tater Tot."

She smiled. "That's good because a dog collar isn't my style."

"You should look in the box again and see if that is your style."

There was something else? And she had missed it? She hurried to open the box again. And that's when she spotted a sapphire pendant on a white-gold chain. She gaped. No one had ever given her something so beautiful.

She looked at him. "Thank you. This is definitely my style."

He smiled at her. "I'm glad you like it. Here. Let me help you put it on."

After she fished it out of the box and unhooked it, she handed it to him. He stepped behind her and hooked the chain. Her fingers pressed against the pendant, which was resting on her chest. It fit her perfectly.

She turned to Colin and lifted on her tiptoes and pressed her lips to his. At first, he didn't move, as though she'd caught him off guard. But as she deepened the kiss, he kissed her back. Her heart pitter-pattered. Her arms reached up and snaked around the back of his neck, pulling him closer to her. She could get used to this.

The door opened, and they jumped apart. She glanced over to see Justin come rushing out. He was moving so fast she wasn't even sure he'd seen them.

"Hey, Justin, where are you going?" Colin called out.

"I have something to do." He moved toward his pickup.

"But it's Christmas."

Justin didn't look back, nor did he slow down. He jumped into his pickup. He fired up the engine and drove away.

Holly looked at Colin. "Any idea what's going on with him?"

"If I was a betting man, I'd wager it has something to do with Felicity."

"Felicity?" She turned to see Justin's pickup before it turned out of sight. "Are those two back together?"

Colin shrugged. "Your guess is as good as mine."

"Interesting. Very interesting."

Join Holly and Colin as they take the next big step in their relationship! Sign-up for my newsletter and receive a Bonus Epilogue. Get your bonus epilogue HERE or visit my website at JenniferFaye.com

Then return to Kringle Falls, Vermont, for the final story in this charming holiday series... PUPPY HUGS & MISTLETOE KISSES. Join Felicity Wright as she loses her job and returns to Kringle Falls. While keeping her unemployment a secret, Felicity is paired with her ex-boyfriend, Justin Bishop, to work on the

town's Christmas play. It's going to be a bumpy journey to a New Year!

Afterword

Thanks so much for reading Holly and Colin's story. I hope their journey made your heart smile. If you did enjoy the book, please consider...

- Help spreading the word about PUPPY SMOOCHES & PEPPERMINT KISSES by writing a review.
- Subscribe to my newsletter in order to receive information about my next release as well as find out about giveaways and special sales.
- You can like my author page on Facebook or follow me on Bookbub.

I hope you'll visit Kringle Falls, Vermont again for the next book in the series, PUPPY HUGS & MISTLETOE KISSES. You don't want to miss updates on previous characters and their love interest.

Coming next is Felicity Wright and Justin Bishop's story...

Thanks again for your support! It is HUGELY appreciated.

Happy reading,
Jennifer

ABOUT AUTHOR

Award-winning author, Jennifer Faye pens fun, heartwarming contemporary romances. With more than a million books sold, she is internationally published with books translated into more than a dozen languages and her work has been optioned for film. She is a two-time winner of the RT Book Reviews Reviewers' Choice Award, the CataRomance Reviewers' Choice Award, named a TOP PICK author, and been nominated for numerous other awards.

Now living her dream, she resides with her very patient husband with a spoiled kitty and a pampered pooch. When she's not plotting out her next romance, you can find her curled up with a mug of tea and a book. You can learn more about Jennifer at www.JenniferFaye.com

Subscribe to Jennifer's newsletter for news about upcoming releases, bonus content and other special offers.

You can also join her on Bookbub, Facebook, or Goodreads.

Also By

Other titles available by Jennifer Faye include:

BLUESTAR ISLAND:
Love Blooms
Harvest Dance
A Lighthouse Café Christmas
Rising Star
Summer by the Beach
Brass Anchor Inn
Summer Refresh
A Seaside Bookshop Christmas
A Lighthouse Snapshot
Inheriting Her Island House
A Brass Anchor Inn Christmas
Race to the Beach
The Art of Seashells – coming soon

KRINGLE FALLS:
Puppy Wishes & Candy Kisses
Puppy Love & Snowflake Kisses

Puppy Smooches & Peppermint Kisses
Puppy Hugs & Mistletoe Kisses – coming soon

THE BAYBERRY, VERMONT SERIES:
Christmas in Bayberry
Valentine's in Bayberry
Rumors in Bayberry
Springtime in Bayberry – coming soon

SEABREEZE WEDDING CHAPEL:
The Bride's Dream Wedding
The Bride's Pink Shoes
The Bride's Christmas Dress
The Runaway Bride's Vow
The Bride's Antique Ring

WHISTLE STOP ROMANCE SERIES:
A Moment to Love
A Moment to Dance
A Moment on the Lips
A Moment to Cherish
A Moment at Christmas

TANGLED CHARMS:
Sprinkled with Love
A Mistletoe Kiss

GREEK PARADISE ESCAPE:
Greek Heir to Claim Her Heart
It Started with a Royal Kiss
Second Chance with the Bridesmaid

WEDDING BELLS IN LAKE COMO:
Bound by a Ring & a Secret

Falling for Her Convenient Groom

ONCE UPON A FAIRYTALE:
Beauty & Her Boss
Miss White & the Seventh Heir
Fairytale Christmas with the Millionaire

THE BARTOLINI LEGACY:
The Prince and the Wedding Planner
The CEO, the Puppy & Me
The Italian's Unexpected Heir

GREEK ISLAND BRIDES:
Carrying the Greek Tycoon's Baby
Claiming the Drakos Heir
Wearing the Greek Millionaire's Ring

Click HERE to find all of Jennifer's titles and buy link or visit JenniferFaye.com

Made in United States
Troutdale, OR
11/16/2025

41995273R00146